EDGE OF INTEGRITY

A Terry McGuire Thriller

ARTHUR COLE &
NIGEL C. WILLIAMS

WORDCATCHER publishing

Edge of Integrity
A Terry McGuire Thriller – Book 2

© 2016-19 Arthur Cole & Nigel C. Williams
Source images supplied by Adobe Stock
Cover design © 2019 David Norrington

British Library Cataloguing in Publication Data.
A catalogue record for this book is available from the British Library.

Published in the United Kingdom by Wordcatcher Publishing Group Ltd
www.wordcatcher.com
Tel: 02921 888321
Facebook.com/WordcatcherPublishing

First Edition: 2016, published by Artcymru Publications
Second Edition: 2019, Wordcatcher Publishing, revised and re-edited

Print edition ISBN: 9781789420678
Ebook edition ISBN: 9781789420685

Category: Crime Thriller

Terry McGuire Thriller Series

Unethical Conduct
Edge of Integrity
Death and Depravity
Angel of Death
Nest of Vipers
Night Hawker
Redemption
Betrayal

Coming Soon
Raven Conner Investigates

TERRY MCGUIRE GLOSSARY

ACC	Assistant Chief Constable
antecedents	history – background records
B&B	Bed and breakfast
bach	Welsh term of endearment; literally, *small*
Bramshill	Police Staff College for ranks of Inspector and above
Bramshill Flyer	an officer entering the service as a constable whilst holding a degree and selected for accelerated promotion through the ranks
brasses	prostitutes
butt, butty, bud	friend, pal, chum
CID	Criminal Investigation Department
collator	an experienced constable updating and maintaining records of crimes and events of interest to officers
CPS	Crown Prosecution Service
CRO	Criminal Record Office
cwtsch	cuddle/hug
DC	Detective Constable
DCI	Detective Chief Inspector
DI	Detective Inspector
DNA	Deoxyribonucleic acid
dob / grass someone up	to inform on someone
DS	Detective Sergeant
DSS	Department of Social Security
ETA	Estimated Time of Arrival
follow-car	the unit deployed to track behind the target vehicle
GBH	Grievous Bodily Harm
ICU	Intensive Care Unit
IOU	I Owe You
KLM	Dutch National Airline
MISPER	Missing Person Report
MOT	Ministry of Transport certificate of roadworthiness
obs	observations
OP	Observation Point
PCSO	Police Civilian Support Officer

PPI	Policy Protection Insurance
QT	on the quiet / in secrecy
RAF	Royal Air Force
SB	Special Branch
scrotes	undesirables
SOCO	Scene of Crime Officer
SP	Starting Price – slang for 'what's happening?'
Super	Superintendent
Toms	prostitutes
Tox	Toxicology
TWOC	Taking Without Owner's Consent
WDC	Woman Detective Constable

CONTENTS

I walked along the busy high street, peering into windows and occasionally checking the new growth appearing under my nose and on my chin. I had sported a moustache for best part of thirty years but had recently removed it in a moment of madness. Now I was growing it back with the addition of a hairy extension that some called a goatee. Why people called it a goatee, I had no idea. Probably had something to do with the beards of goats, I surmised. My fledgling growth had white flecks of hair that had not been present in the original moustache I'd removed. At least the new growth was matching the snowy flecks at my temples. I had taken to keeping my hair cropped short to match the length of the thinning thatch on top and I wondered how long it would take for the rest of it to lose its colour. Would any be left on top by the time the follicles failed to make any pigment? But then again, did it really matter? Not now, for sure. Perhaps thirty years ago? Definitely thirty years ago. Ageing had its obvious pitfalls, but the fading of ego and narcissistic tendencies that accompanied advancing years was, for me, a good thing that everybody needed to experience.

I strolled easily into the shopping mall in the centre of Cardiff city, I tried to maintain a casual stride and confident swing of my arms that matched my appearance of a man in some middle-management role, making the most of his morning break. The more I thought about being casual the less I felt I was achieving it.

Riding an escalator to the first-floor atrium of the precinct, the large apple sign above a slick, brushed aluminium and glass, computer shop drew me in. The Sirens of consumerism, the evil, false beauties of the oceans of retail finance drawing the money-laden, technology-loving Argonauts to their financial doom at the bottom of the digital briny with the analogue loan sharks.

The store was cleverly designed to maximise the impact of the product design. I could appreciate the planning and research that must have gone into every last detail as I stared at each oversized retail altar laden with the electronic objects to be sacrificed to the wishful congregation, hustling for attention before the temple priests dedicated to the word of the great Lord Job.

Pushing through the crowd, I peered over the last line of shoppers playing with the iPad demonstrators and caught a glimpse of the price of ownership for one of the technological marvels. "Fuck me!" I said, too loud, then realised all the faces around me were looking at me with distaste, all except a teenage boy who thought it was hilarious.

"Sorry," I said as I slipped sheepishly back towards the exit.

As I walked out the door, something caught my eye. Sitting on a bench twenty metres away was a twenty-something man I knew I had seen before. It was nobody I had seen before today, but this was the third time I had seen him in the last ten minutes. Coincidence? Possibly. But I didn't believe in coincidence. The man was reading a newspaper, the same newspaper I had seen him reading earlier whilst he was leaning against a wall near the Apple shop.

I was suddenly aware of other eyes avoiding direct contact with me. A young woman walked towards me and I stepped out in front of her, deliberately. Strangely, she didn't look at me, merely changed her course and walked on. That was not normal. Even the timidest of people would have muttered an apology, even if it wasn't their fault.

I took the escalator again and this time rode it to the ground floor. I wanted to run but didn't want to overreact. I had to be sure I was being followed before making my move.

Stepping off the moving stairs, I walked to a bench where I sat for a moment – a four-place bench, made from highly varnished thick strips of some wood bent into an ergonomic shape that I felt looked better than it was to sit on. The handcuffs I carried in a pouch on my belt dug into my side and I had to slide the holder along my belt to a spot where it no longer bothered me. I had often been teased for still carrying handcuffs wherever I went on duty. As a senior officer it was argued that I no longer needed them. There were others, lower in rank that would do the real policing. But I would never part with them. I felt they kept me connected to the real job, the job of constable, the job I had joined many years before.

A casually dressed couple approached stopped at the window of a shop opposite me. The man was tall and slim. I guessed he was measuring in at six feet tall and weighing in around twelve stone. He looked fit and like someone who liked to play sport. The man wasn't wearing a coat over his tight-fitting jumper, so he had either parked his car in the multi-storey car park that formed part of the shopping mall or had a clear plan which did not include leaving the warmth and dry mall at all. But the woman with him was wearing a coat. It was the type that was made of a material that stopped water soaking through but allowed air in and had a logo emblazoned on the upper arm that suggested it cost a fair penny but would suit someone used to walking the hills and mountains rather than find adventure inside a mall. They had their backs to me, but I could see their eyes in the reflection. They were staring. Their eyes were fixed firmly on me.

It was time to make a move. I stood and walked on towards the mall exit. As I stepped out through the door, I saw another face I recognised from somewhere, aged about thirty, standing to the side of the exit and smoking a cigarette. The smoker looked away as I approached him.

This was it. The smoker spun as I pushed him up against the wall. "If I was your real target you'd be fucked," I growled.

2

Being the new kid on the block is never easy. I remembered the first day at the new schools I had been sent to through the different stages of my youth and how the excitement of the unknown was tempered by the expectation of inevitable friction with some arsehole or other wishing to lay down some ground rules, to establish the hierarchy at the outset. I was nowhere near a kid anymore, but I was certainly new to the squad of officers assembled before me and if anyone wanted to try to impose their will on me, they would be severely disappointed. I had never stood by and let a bully impose themselves on any of the new groups I had found myself a part of as a kid and I certainly had no intention of letting it happen now at this stage in my life and career.

The team had been together for some time and that meant they had an advantage over me; that always made me feel uneasy. I already knew that they needed to improve on their surveillance technique. They had failed to follow me through the shopping mall without being noticed and that was something I could use to begin building trust. A stick before offering the carrot.

Before taking the post as the new Detective Chief Inspector on the drug squad, I had called in to the 'big house' to speak with Alan Chambers, the Assistant Chief Constable for crime.

The headquarters had changed a great deal since I first joined the force, many years before. It wasn't just the unsuccessful make-over of the exterior of the building that had left it looking like mutton dressed as lamb, it was also something, to my mind, far more insidious, a change of thinking and attitude that seemed to infect everyone inside the building. The 'force' had officially become a 'service,' although the vast majority of us in the force already saw ourselves as providing an essential service, we didn't need to have to be labelled with the word as well. Quotas now seemed to be a major factor in the mind-set of those determining suitability for appointment to the office of constable and I sensed that most of the senior officers were more attuned to their personal rise through the ranks than the welfare of their troops.

I had always believed in equality, even before the political classes hijacked it for their own purposes. The police 'service' needed recruits from all sectors of the community. That was just common sense. It mattered not one jot to me what colour, race sex or religion a recruit identified with. As long as they were committed to the job then that was OK with me. But now, with all the budget cuts that had decimated numbers on the beat, essential officers that were being substituted by an increase in numbers of well-meaning but toothless Police Civilian Support Officers, the job was nothing like the one I had signed up for many years ago. It was all just alien to me, and I wondered where it would end.

The Assistant Chief Constable for Crime sat behind his teak desk adorned with silver-framed family photographs and sipped from a corrugated paper Starbucks advert. I wondered what poor sod had been required to do the coffee run when there was a percolator in his office? Perhaps he did a drive through on his way in?

"I'm not even thinking of having a good clean out of the squad," I told him, much to his surprise, "I want to find my feet first and see how the land lies."

He sipped some more over-priced beans and thought for a while. I got the impression he was disappointed. "Guess you're right," he finally sighed. "You can't tar everyone with the same brush. However," he paused for emphasis, "...if the top man was at it, what else may have been going on within the squad?"

I knew he was referring to ex DCI Cliff Ambrose, a man I had arrested and sent to jail for life for murder and corruption. Now it was my time to think long and hard, but my priority had to be the appointment of a new DI before anything else could be done. That would help take pressure off me on a day-to-day basis and would let me weed out the crop of unwanted plants I had inherited. "I've got to have a good right-hand-man, someone I can trust and who'll go the extra mile," I said. "It would also help if he isn't a corrupt bastard," I teased. The ACC nodded but didn't see the funny side. I guessed he was still fielding flak from wood panelled offices way above those playing host to top ranks within the police.

I already knew the bloke I wanted for Detective Inspector. I had sounded him out prior to meeting with Alan Chambers. I hoped it was only going to be a formality to get him on board. I wanted Mike Johns. We went back a long way. He was a career bobby with plenty of CID experience who didn't suffer fools gladly. I'd been on a few high-profile cases with him over the years. He was divorced, through no apparent fault of his own. His kids had grown up, so he had no pressing ties, and had about four years left to serve before retirement. I knew he'd give me a-hundred-and-ten per cent. The dream team, I thought.

Chambers had already moved the previous squad DI on to pastures new. He'd given him the usual fanny about it being better for his career and that it would benefit him to have a fresh start elsewhere, somewhere they'd value his input. Of course, he'd either fallen for it, hook, line and sinker, or accepted it as an escape from what was going to be an uncomfortable experience of answering for the oversight of a multitude of wrongs committed during his watch. This way he would be saving some degree of reputation. I felt this spoke volumes for the bloke. He was obviously a 'look after number one' kind of man. There were more than just a few of those mercenary bastards creeping into the job of late.

Chambers agreed the appointment of Mike Johns and I left for my office.

***

So, the hour had come and now I stood before the team I would be working with for the foreseeable future – it was time to meet and greet.

There were twenty officers in all, eighteen DC's and two DS's. They all seemed a little disillusioned, not surprising really, bearing in mind they had fucked up on the first task I had set them – the surveillance exercise at the mall – lost two of their former leaders in double quick time – one banged up and the other deserting like a rat from a sinking ship. I was determined to steer that ship to safer waters and not let it drift rudderless like the Captain of the Marie Celeste.

I was well aware that it was now my job to raise

the morale of the team and to get them working like a well-oiled machine. I'd had enough experience to know that it might not all be plain sailing. Although I had arranged the exercise at the mall, I had not met any of the team. I didn't want to know what they looked like before the test of their surveillance techniques. I had wanted to assess my own anti-surveillance skills without any advantage.

I had called the briefing to introduce myself and the new DI and was relieved to see Mike John's smiling face at the front of the assembled ranks when the rest of the team had started filing in. I could see the lack of enthusiasm in the eyes of those who dragged their feet, didn't smile and didn't even talk amongst themselves.

I introduced Mike and me to the team and set out my ideas for the way forward, my *vision* for the future of the squad. They must have all thought I had snorted something illicit; I was wound up like a coiled spring. It was a new chapter for them and for me – bring it on.

I made a point of not mentioning former DCI Cliff Ambrose's name during the briefing, why should I? They all knew the score, he was corrupt, he took his chances and he got potted, end of story. That was the way it went and they were all very aware of that. They were also very much aware that I was the man responsible for putting the bent bastard behind bars.

I didn't really go into a lot of depth with them. I

did all the talking about my vision and they just listened.

I knew I'd have to spend time with them to get to really know them. I believed a person could learn more about someone else when having a one-to-one with them. That would come. I fully intended on having chats with every member of the team.

I re-enforced what I wanted from them: dedication, honesty, integrity and a strong work ethic – basic principles of decent policing, something that I knew was missing during Cliff's rein.

I told them that I'd be having the private chats with each of them in due course. I then told all the DC's to crack on with their existing duties. The two DS's were told to stay behind. I wanted them to bring Mike and me up to speed on the current enquiries the squad were involved in, but I already knew they weren't doing a lot. I intended to change that. I believed in pro-active policing, not just reactive.

I had known the two detective sergeants, Steve Thompson and Colin Anderson, for many years. I knew they were two hard working detectives who had been involved in the drug scene for most of their service. I had Steve's number saved in my phone and had called him a couple of days ago and told him I wanted the team to try and follow me through the city centre without me being aware of their presence. They had failed. Steve had been spitting bullets when I pinned one of his DC's against the mall wall. He told me he would tear strips off them for being so sloppy and that they'd spend the days practising to get it right before I arrived.

I now needed to know how my incumbent sergeants felt about my appointment and if they still had the commitment to bring major villains to book with me in charge.

Colin Anderson had seemed happiest to speak first. "I don't know what you've heard about us, boss? But there are some good officers here. None of us had any proof of what Cliff was really up to, honest! We suspected something, didn't we, Steve?"

Steve Thompson agreed. "We all suspected he was a bit warm but none of us had any proof. Neither of us would have sat back and let him continue if we could have proved it." He produced a tattered notebook from his jacket pocket. "This is just some of the stuff Colin and I were collecting on the bastard. If you hadn't done him, I'm sure we'd have got him in the end. I'd heard a rumour from a nark about him, but you know how unreliable they can be, especially without hard evidence."

I nodded. Their leader had put them in an unacceptable position and if they were telling me the truth, I could understand their predicament. I had to take them on face value – the notebook helped.

"I don't know how this squad has been run," I said, "but there are going to be a few changes," I warned them. "You two will play an important part in the future, if you want to, that is. Cliff was a bad bastard and for the life of me I cannot fathom out how he got away with his shit for so long. This is going to be a new era for our squad and together we can take it forward at a great rate of knots, are you ready for the ride, gentlemen?"

They looked at each other, nodding their heads in agreement. I saw a crack of a smile appear on Steve's face and then I stood, grinned and shook their hands. "Now go back to the troops and tell them in no uncertain terms how I'll be running it. I will not accept any form of corruption. If we lose our integrity, we lose everything. If any of them has a problem with that, they know where the door is."

They left with what I would like to think was a spring in their step. Perhaps I imagined it, perhaps I just wanted to think that, but I knew they got my message.

Mike was grinning. He knew I was just laying the foundations and that good foundations depended upon clear, solid ground, straight lines and clear, readable plans.

"Get all the personnel records of the squad," I said. We had a lot of reading to do before we could get an insight to what we were dealing with.

I couldn't be sure if Mike agreed with my way of working but I knew he understood something drastic had to be done. He also knew that he could share his concerns with me at any time. That was good enough for me and he didn't raise an objection.

3

I'd decided I needed to test the water with the crew. I knew it could all backfire and end up with the team being split and not trusting me, but I had to know who was really with me and who was not.

I'd heard from Colin that he suspected one of the lads was into using steroids in his weight-training regime. That allegation was now on my 'to do' list. The use of steroids was not acceptable for a copper, under any circumstances. The drugs body builders used were illegal and whilst they remained that way there was no way any of my officers would be taking them without severe consequences. But the major worry for me was that three of the team were rumoured to be heavy gamblers. I always tried to stay out of the private lives of my officers, but gambling always led to debts and debts led to leverage for those who had a vested interest in getting IOU's from coppers. It had to end. Gambling could lead to addiction. No kind of addiction was acceptable for officers of the law dealing daily with other addicts.

I called the three men into my office, one at a time. They would be the first in my series of one-to-ones that I'd planned.

Tim Paulett had been a detective for thirteen years and a uniform copper for four years prior to joining the CID. He had a good record. It was littered with complaints from toe-rags, but every senior officer knew that complaints were part and parcel of a good copper's career. I had no problem with that. There was nothing officially logged in his file regarding gambling problems.

Tim sat opposite me. He seemed nervous but not unduly so. I remembered being nervous when I used to meet new bosses.

"I want you to know from the outset, that I've heard you like to gamble," I said and I held up my hand to stop him interrupting. "Gambling creates debts and debts lead to trouble. Before you reply, let me tell you that I do *not* accept liars in my team. You can lie to anyone else, but you *never* lie to me. Do you understand?"

He nodded his head. I could see him start to say something but think better of it.

"Now, I'm not asking you to admit to gambling. I don't want you to get yourself into a position where you might be tempted to break my rule. I am simply telling you straight that as from this moment on you will never gamble again whilst you work for me."

"I understand, sir," he said.

"If I hear one word about you even betting on a fly climbing a wall your arse will be out that door faster than a virgin running from John Holmes. Do I make myself clear?"

"Yes, sir. Perfectly clear."

"Are you going to remain part of my team?"

He didn't think about it. "Yes, sir. I'd like to, if you'll have me?"

I stood and shook his hand. "Welcome on board."

My one-to-one with Dave Matthews went pretty much the same way, but the last interview, with DC Karl Dixon, was a completely different experience.

I told him the same thing I told the others but when I asked him if he wanted to remain a part of the team, he had a meltdown.

"Who the fuck do you think you are?" he shouted at me. "How dare you speak to me about my private life? What I do in my time off is up to me, as long as I'm not breaking the law," he quickly added.

My immediate reaction was to kick his arse out of the door, but I sensed this was more than just interference into his private affairs.

I took a stab. "How much do you owe?" I said quietly.

He looked dumbstruck. He began to sneer. His mouth began to work without sounds. I watched as his expression morphed through a range of emotions, then I saw the first of the tears stream down his face.

I said nothing. I left him there alone for a

moment and brought back two cups of coffee.

He looked surprised. "Go on," I said. "Best office coffee I've ever tasted."

He wiped his face with the back of his hand and took the drink.

We sat quietly for a moment.

"Four grand," he finally whispered, as if saying it quietly would make it seem less real.

I said nothing.

He drank some more of his coffee. "Not to loan sharks, just the bank, but the bank is refusing to extend my overdraft and I can't see any other way out but to keep on trying to win it back."

"You know that won't happen, don't you? It never does work out well. It's how they get you hooked. The hope that the next bet will be the one that turns things around. You understand why we can't let you go on like this?"

He nodded his head.

I felt sorry for him. I had read his file and knew he had divorced recently. It couldn't have been easy.

"Look," I said, "I'm glad you told me, but it's got to stop."

"I know, boss, but I just don't know what to do. Half my money goes to my ex-wife and daughter... Don't get me wrong, I don't begrudge them the money, but I'm constantly overdrawn and it gets worse each month and I can't get out of it."

"It puts us both in an awkward position," I said.

Again, he nodded. I could see the turmoil in his eyes, the struggle of a man who had admitted something that potentially could cost him his career. It hadn't taken much to get him to confess, a few well-chosen, firm words that left him in no doubt that he would be found out if he chose to lie. If only the criminals were so accommodating, but I knew only too well that DC Karl Dixon was no criminal and that he was crying out for help. He had found himself in a terrible place, a place he believed would end his dreams and aspirations and it had all gone too far, too far for him to deal with on his own. He needed someone to confess to, someone to listen to him, even if it meant the end of his career.

I thought for a moment. "Let me see what we can work out for you."

He looked shocked. "Am I sacked, boss?"

"At the very least, you should be winging your way back to division," I warned him. "But stay with us for the time being, until we can work something out. Perhaps it'll all turn out OK."

He shook his head. "I can't see how."

"All I ask from you is an assurance that there'll be no more gambling. If you can give me that assurance then there'll be a place here for you. Can you promise me there'll be no more?"

He nodded slowly then looked me straight in the eyes. "Yes, sir. I give you my word that I'll do whatever it takes. I can't go on like this. I want it to go away."

I saw the honesty, the fragility in his face, the little boy hoping for someone to pick him up and cuddle him and to tell him everything will be alright. The truth was, I didn't know if things would be alright and I certainly wasn't going to pick him up and cuddle him. But I did feel for him. I let him tidy himself up before he left my office. I had no way of knowing if he'd stick to his promise, but I had a feeling that he would. At least I hoped he would.

I checked through his personal file again. Every police officer gets a personal file or record that accompanies them through their career. It logs their personal details, their marital situation or otherwise, their qualifications, their postings, complaints made against them and commendations for work considered to be exemplary or above and beyond the call of duty. The record was used to determine suitability for certain roles and even for promotion interviews or 'boards' as we called them. I looked at the photo on the front page, a proud, young version of the DC that had aged beyond his years due to worry that was self-inflicted to a great extent. Karl had ten years' service, fifteen commendations. Four of those were Chief Superintendent commendations and the rest were the best type awarded by the Chief Constable –

impressive, if that kind of thing impresses you. He was also qualified to sergeant. He had a glowing future ahead of him, if he could sort himself out.

I knew from experience that team management was more than just allocating and directing resources. Sometimes it took a little empathy, to understand that not everyone has the same breaks in life and that we all have to find ways to make it through the day.

I didn't know what I could do for Karl, but I was sure as hell going to do the best I could.

4

I made enquiries with the force welfare officer and the federation representative to see if there was anything we could do for an anonymous officer in debt. There was no way I was going to divulge his identity. Perhaps, if I truly was a team player then I should have informed my bosses, but I knew there'd be a marker added to Karl's personal record that would have lasting and possibly devastating outcomes. I was glad to hear that there was a chance of sorting an emergency, interest free loan for him from the welfare fund and perhaps arranging a collection from the troops force-wide. I asked them both to look into it further.

I'd just received a pay rise for my promotion and knew that I had a few quid to spare, not that my wife Molly would agree with that assessment of our financial situation. We were always on the edge of our overdraft, living month to month on an agreement with the bank that charged us a crippling rate for something we didn't want but had no option in accepting and, indeed, accepting with a sycophantic smile.

I'd kick-start something with a discreet collection within the squad. It would be interesting to see who would respond favourably and who would refuse to contribute. I'd worked with lots of tight-arsed coppers over the years but knew that everyone's circumstances were different, and circumstances dictated attitudes to charity. Some people simply didn't have money to spare.

I tasked Karl Dixon with a trawl of the files; it was as much an effort to take his mind off his trouble as it was to prioritise forthcoming actions.

A trawl of files wasn't something that many liked to do but he smiled at me when I asked him to do it. I could see he knew my true motivation behind the request. I needed him to just think about the job, to block out his worries and problems, something I knew only too well was often impossible to do. But a detective had to be focused on the job, sometimes lives depended on it and, with drugs at the epicentre of our remit, lives were often depending on us, even when those involved in the despicable trade had no idea of that dependence on us. I had always believed that anything we could do to stop one person becoming an addict, or removing dangerous drugs from circulation, would be a small step in the right direction. At least that's what I thought as I began my new job.

5

Turner carried a large, brand name, plastic shopping bag through the mall like hundreds of others looking for bargains on any day of any week. But Turner was not like other shoppers. Turner had no intention of paying for anything he took a fancy to. Inside the large plastic bag was a large empty box with the top cut away to allow easy access to the empty space within. He was dressed like any other shopper. He kept a good pair of jeans and a neat designer top for his shopping trips. They were what he called his 'work clothes'. He had to look just like any of the other consumers packing the Cardiff mall.

He stopped outside a store selling the latest designs of a high-end clothing line and entered. The subdued lighting and narrow aisles made it a shoplifter's paradise. Packed with potential customers, the staff relied heavily on CCTV to spot thieves, primarily after the event, but Turner knew that the confined conditions and bustling shoppers were a hindrance for any conscientious or self-respecting security guard. Funky interior design had become king at the expense of security and even safety in some places. Turner wondered how anyone would ever get out of the place if a fire broke out. What the hell, it had nothing to do with him.

He spotted a hoody that cost more than all his benefits for a week. He picked it off the shelf and held it up to a low-wattage overhead light. He made a grimace and folded it again before replacing it on the top of the pile. He was about to walk off, as if uninterested in the garment, but he made a quick visual check of the faces around him and then knocked the garment into the open topped box within his carrier bag. Nobody had seen the move; of that he was sure. Perhaps a camera somewhere had picked it up but by the time someone saw the footage, and did something about it, Turner would be miles away. He carried on strolling around the shop, adding a pair of extortionate jeans and three T-shirts.

Shopping done, Turner left the store and walked out of the plaza to a pre-determined location behind a nearby church where he knew CCTV was absent, one of the few places in the city centre where the all-seeing eyes were yet to be installed. It was only a matter of time before that changed.

A small man in designer tracksuit and track shoes stood against a corner of the church. Turner saw him blow a thick cloud of white smoke from one of the vaporisers that seemed to be popular with smokers these days. Turner preferred the real thing. The smell from the vape was some kind of fruit, he guessed at blueberry, a pleasant aroma that seemed somehow out of place. The guy in the tracksuit nodded to Turner as he walked towards him. The fence took the bag from Turner, tipped the contents into a holdall and then and handed the bag back, along with forty quid for his troubles. It wasn't a lot, considering he was taking all the risks, but it was enough to make a difference.

***

Brian Turner flicked the switch to the single pendant light and saw the mess that was his living room. Discarded boxes of pizza and empty cans of beer littered the floor. It had been a hell of night. He would clear the rubbish at some time but today he had more pressing matters. He tucked his special shopping bag in a cupboard, ready for the next trip to the mall.

The forty quid he had earned from his shopping mission had gone towards his fix. He closed the curtains and set the television to a music channel. His 'kit' was ready, and he assembled the gear on the cluttered coffee table.

He thought of his mother. She had been horrified when she discovered he used heroin and any other drug he could get his hands on. Like most kids dabbling in drugs, he'd started with a bit of blow at the age of fourteen because his mates were into it. He was only too aware of the circumstances behind his decline. He knew that all the bollocks about cannabis not being a gateway drug was just that – bollocks. The drug itself might not be a gateway to harder stuff but it had brought him into contact with the dealer who soon pushed him onto the harder stuff. Brian Turner was very much aware of all this, but it made no difference, he was hooked. There was no going back for him.

His mother had thrown him out of the family home when he had begun to feed his addiction by stealing money from her purse. He knew she had tried to help him, but nothing was more important to him than his fix – not even his family. He missed his little brother. His mother hadn't forbidden him from seeing Chris but Brian didn't want his little bro' seeing him in a state. He wanted more for his brother and the only way he could contribute to that was by staying away. Brian often wondered where he would be if he'd stayed off the drugs but, like anyone with an addiction, he had spent his life justifying the use of drugs, calling for the legalisation of cannabis. Justification was abdication of responsibility. Brian knew this. He had come to realise that he was tired of living like this. He wanted to change. He had heard people say that acceptance of being an addict was the first step in recovery. At least that's what they said about those who drank too much. Perhaps he was at that point where he could change. He accepted the fact that he was an addict. He accepted that what he had done was wrong. He accepted, at long last, that he had been the author of his own misfortune. That particular acceptance had been a bitch to take but he knew he couldn't blame anyone other than himself and his so-called friends for getting into drugs. Fact.

This couldn't go on. He had to stop – somehow.

***

Carol Parker knocked at the door to the rented flat. She was shaking and in need of a fix. Brian had called her and told her to come around. Now he wasn't answering the door. She knocked again but still there was no answer. She remembered the spare key that Brian hid in the rotten doorframe. He was probably already off his face.

She pulled the key from its hiding place. The door stuck on its frame but a sharp shove just below the lock always did the trick. The light was on in the stairwell leading up to the living room.

"Hi, Bri,' it's only me," she called.

No reply.

She walked into the living room. The gear was on the coffee table. Brian was probably in the bedroom, sleeping off the hit.

Carol walked to the table to check on the gear. Perhaps he'd left some for her. Then she froze. Brian lay between the settee and the coffee table. His eyes were open but sightless, dry and lacking the life that once shone through them. Carol was in no doubt that Brian Turner was dead.

***

I got the call about a death in a council owned flat in a street off Cowbridge Road West in Ely, Cardiff.

I got Karl Dixon to drive me down to the address to interview the girl who had called in the discovery of what appeared to be an overdose.

I would normally let the lads sort something like this out themselves, but, being new to the squad, I wanted to get my hands dirty.

The flat was on the second floor of a recently refurbished two-storey town house. Owned by the council, the outside looked attractively decorated with new paint and windows, but I noticed that the side door leading to the upper flat had yet to be replaced. The wooden frame had rotted, and the door wasn't in much better condition. It was now a possible crime scene. We were pretty sure the death was as a result of an overdose, but it never paid to be careless or to assume anything. Scenes of Crime had already done the business and Geoff, a scenes of crime officer with more years' experience digging around in bodies than Hannibal Lector, met us on the stairs. "Looks like an overdose to me, Terry. Don't think anyone else was involved. Mind you, it would be impossible to tell if there was. Place is full of all kinds of shit."

We passed Geoff and entered the lounge to find

the body of a young man being loaded into a black plastic body bag by two guys in black suits. Going by their physiques and general appearance, they were more like 'Happy Feet' than the 'Men in Black.' I stopped the penguins and took a look at the victim. He was no older than my son, perhaps a year or two younger. I wondered what his family would do when they found out? I knew how I'd react at such a wasted life but in cases like these it was never a certainty. Most of the public think druggies are down-and-outs, people cast out from home to become social pariahs. But experience is enlightening. I'd seen people from all walks of life, plumbers, secretaries, even solicitors, coppers and Members of Parliament addicted to the shit. The perception of drugs being a recreational activity couldn't be further from the truth. Drugs ruined lives and all users either discovered that for themselves or ended up paying the ultimate price like the young lad now on his way to the morgue.

6

It had been a quiet afternoon in the Special Branch office at Cardiff airport, not that it was ever busy if compared to the big airports like Heathrow or Gatwick. It was a good time to make arrangements and to check those already made for a forthcoming joint operation with the people from immigration.

Detective Sergeant Aled Powell ran a hand through his thinning red hair and sipped his coffee as he stood at his desk staring at the computer screen. He was trying not to look at John Snaith, a rather odd-looking member of the immigration team, who stood to one side and was busily rearranging his wedding tackle for the umpteenth time in less than ten minutes.

"For crying out loud. Go to the bog and sort yourself out. It's distracting and putting me off my coffee," Aled Powell said. "I don't want to see you playing with your bollocks."

Snaith shook his head. "Don't know what's wrong? Been itching and burning for a couple of days. Playing hell with me."

"It's hardly going to be a dose of pox, now is it?" Powell teased. "No self-respecting bird is going to shag you."

Snaith let it go. Powell knew he would. They were always ribbing each other and Snaith gave as good as he got. It was part of the job. Not politically correct but great fun – most of the time. The humour within emergency service staff could often be mistaken for callous and even sick at times but the job demanded a certain kind of behaviour even at the most dreadful of scenes and Snaith and Powell were no different from others in their belief that the humour was what kept them going each day.

"Seriously... go and see about it. Might be something bad, like bollock cancer or something."

"Oh, thanks very much. You know how to make a bloke feel at ease."

"You'll be thanking me if it saves your life."

Snaith shrugged. "I'll go and see the quack after this job's finished." Snaith was average-build with a head that seemed too big for his body, inevitably leading to his nickname of Mister Potato Head.

A joint operation had been planned for the airport for the following week. The immigration service had received information that a target would be flying into Cardiff from Sierra Leone via Schiphol. This person would be in possession of a number of forged passports and documentation. The dodgy documents were bound for the London suburbs and would be sold on at a decent profit.

The office phone rang, and Powell picked up. "Information desk. DS Powell required urgently," the voice said. He hung up and made his way to the desk in the departures lounge where a smiling face directed him to one of the local taxi drivers standing next to a cab at the entrance to the terminal. Powell and his small team had cultivated a good relationship with the drivers of the local cab company. If they ever had information that they thought might be important, Powell was the go-to man.

Khaled had parked his cab in a no-stop zone. It always looked good to be seen to be having a bollocking off one of the local coppers when, in fact, he was passing information that he knew kept him on their good side.

The cab driver had come to Wales from Iraq twenty-six years ago, during the first Iraq war. He'd settled in well and saw himself as Welsh, he wore the same Welsh rugby jersey every day during the seven weeks of the rugby internationals and wore a Welsh Rugby Union tie during every other shift he worked. The internationals were some weeks off in the future so the tie was the order of the day. He even had an odd Welsh accent that Powell found amusing but heart-warming. The man wanted to be seen to belong, to be part of his new country. Powell guessed his time in the country had not always been as accepting as it should, especially in more recent times with the growth of the far-rightwing extremists peddling hatred through any media outlet they could access.

"What's up?" Powell asked Khaled. That tie had to be changed soon, Powell could see a full range of ingredients from Khaled's favourite menu ingrained within its fibres.

"Just saw two big dealers from Barry in the airport, Detective Powell. Got no luggage and I seen them heading up to the restaurant."

"How do you know them?"

"Picked them up from a pub one-night last year. They were pissed and I heard them talking. When I got back to office, I show other drivers my Go-Pro film. They tell me they big dealers, mun." Powell almost laughed when he heard Khaled add 'mun' to the end of his sentence. It was a uniquely Welsh throwaway word that seemed equal in use to that of 'butt' in certain parts of the Principality.

"Have you still got the video?"

He shook his head. "When I realise what they are talking about, I get scared and rub it away."

"You erased it?"

"Yes, erased. It records over it, mun, you understand?"

Powell got the driver to flick on his hazard lights and to lock his cab. They walked together through the quiet departures area and took the escalator up to the restaurant on the first floor of the terminal where the cabbie discreetly identified the dealers.

Returning to the Special Branch office, Powell

sat and focused on the bank of CCTV screens that filled a small corner of the office. The smell of freshly percolating coffee was a temptation he couldn't resist. He knew he had to cut down on the caffeine but sometimes the pressure of work dictated a constant top-up. He poured a fresh cup with no milk and sat before the monitors.

The two druggies were busily eating their lunch. He zoomed the camera control and could see one getting stuck into a lasagne; the other was scoffing a big plate of fish and chips. The pair of them didn't seem to have a care in the world. They smiled and laughed and looked like a pair off on some holiday somewhere away from the South Wales weather.

Powell's partner, DC Frank Earl had returned from a staff appraisal at the headquarters in Bridgend and was quickly brought up to speed. Earl was in a good mood so Powell assumed his staff appraisal must have gone well.

Earl began checking all the incoming flights, particularly from Europe that afternoon. Most flights to and from Cardiff were the 'bucket and spade' types – in and out of Spanish resorts. Not much else passed through of any significant interest.

Special Branch CCTV coverage of the airport, both inside and out, was second to none. It had to be good, with all the terrorism nonsense going on.

The government and security services had used the fear from their paranoia to win a massive investment in upgrades and had spent millions countrywide on state-of-the-art CCTV at all airports throughout the UK. Powell swore, to those who would listen, that the systems were so good you could even see an ant having a piss.

Although Cardiff has never been a busy airport, at certain times of the year it did have its peaks, but not today. Summer holidays, chartered flights and specials for rugby internationals were the bread and butter business. Lots of initiatives had been tried but failed over the years due to a poor transport infrastructure to the airport. No rail link and single-track roads in some places made the airport a nightmare to reach at times. There were many bodies still lobbying the Welsh Assembly and British Government to get urgent upgrades made but the excuse was always a lack of money in times of austerity.

Powell checked the incoming flights. Only one flight was due in soon and that was the KLM from Schiphol with an ETA as expected.

The Dutch city of Amsterdam had a reputation of attracting tourists who liked to puff on joints of wacky backy in cafés, of dope pushers profiting from tourists eager to experience legalised cannabis and the draw of legal prostitution displayed like new designer dresses in shop windows. But the reality of the city can be far removed from the stereotype. Amsterdam is also a city of wonderful architecture and canals, of good food and roadside cafés and culture. It also had historical importance, the city once being one of the foremost trading centres of the world and it was still the largest distributor of oil in Europe. It was all a matter of perspective and Powell's perspective had to remain firmly focused on the seedier end of the city's reputation.

Powell brought Snaith up to speed on the druggies and within fifteen minutes a joint operation was organised. Other collaborating agencies envied the working relationship between the Special Branch and the Immigration people at the airport and Powell and Snaith had played a big part in the development of that relationship.

The KLM A330 Airbus landed on time, about half an hour later, and the two druggies had made their way downstairs to the Arrivals area. It didn't take Sherlock Holmes to deduce that they were meeting somebody off the flight.

It was nearly fifteen minutes before the passengers offloaded and Snaith took up position at the Customs check point to scrutinise the incoming passengers.

Frank Earl had set one of the cameras in Arrivals area to focus on the passport details. There were only ten passengers on the plane and, as sure as eggs is eggs, the druggies were meeting with one of them. He wasn't a stereotypical business commuter, nor was he a typical looking tourist. Aged about forty, wearing a three-quarter length, black leather coat, he was sporting one those fashionable full-beards and wearing a fedora. He looked like a throwback to a character from The Godfather, certainly not someone who wanted to pass through unnoticed.

Powell watched the monitors as the traveller shook the hands of the two druggies and all three made their way to the car park where they got into a top of the range silver BMW 7 Series.

Powell shook his head as he made a note of the registration number of the car. It was a personalised number plate, D 10 PE. "Talk about taking the piss," Powell said to no one in particular. "Who's the beardie-bastard?"

The car drove off and Powell played back the video from the CCTV and crosschecked with the passenger manifesto. The beardie-bastard was a Dutch national by the name of Joost Van Gerber, born in Maastricht.

Powell and Earls knew Van Gerber was unlikely to be visiting a long-lost Welsh grandmother. This could be something big, a break in the drug supply trade that was well overdue. Customs had been pruned back at the airport and Powell wasn't sure they would be too helpful under the circumstances.

There was a chance they could catch the Dutchman and the contacts red-handed if he now made the right decision. The work of the Customs seemed to be more and more reliant upon intelligence. This particular intelligence was police generated, so Powell was determined the police would have ownership of whatever was to come.

***

I got the call and immediately sent Mike and Steve directly to the airport to confer with DS Aled Powell and sort things out down there. I had the rest of the team to speak to and wondered what other issues I would uncover. An effective team had to be a happy team and the squad were anything but that at the moment.

My sergeants were running through a review of outstanding cases with the team. There were some expressions of animosity towards me as I entered the team room and listened to feedback offered for each of the cases being appraised.

Time for more *one-to-ones*.

***

The two officers arrived at the airport within the hour and met with Powell, Earls and John – the immigration guy.

It was all ready for them; three witness statements, copies of all the relevant CCTV – *Happy days*.

Mike thanked Powell and confirmed his thinking that it was perhaps best to keep Customs out of it, at least for a while.

7

Mike and Steve returned from the airport with all the relevant statements and the CCTV footage.

"Are the Customs aware of this?" I asked.

"Not a fucking clue, boss," Mike said. He clearly didn't care either.

I felt the tingle of excitement I usually felt when presented with a new case. We had two well known drug dealers, responsible for much of the shit flowing into South Wales and into the arms or up the noses of our kids and now they had met a dodgy-looking bloke from Amsterdam. Might not be anything in it. Could have been a long-lost relative or a friend from their past but the tingle in my body screamed out to me that it was something we couldn't ignore.

"Well, we'll keep it that way," I said. "I have history with them. I sometimes wonder what side they're on. Steve? Get the identities of the two druggies from Barry, the registered owner details of the car and any other intelligence that may be forthcoming on the pair of bastards."

I turned to Mike. "I want the full SP on the twat from Holland... and we need a name for the operation." I let the team think on that for a moment. "This enquiry is now priority," I continued. "Anything else goes on the back burner, and that isn't much by the look of the files," I grumbled.

We were off and running and I knew it would probably take a few days to get all the background. It gave me time to call in the team and have a little 'off the record' chinwag with rest of them.

I had already been through all the personal records of the DC's on the squad, so I set aside the following day to speak to those I hadn't yet caught up with.

The meetings went well, on the whole. They seemed like a good bunch, but the feedback that I was getting didn't bode too well. In confidence, a few of them mentioned Cliff. They had hardly ever seen him and there had been no direction within the squad, it had all been a disjointed and a mess. That was no surprise.

They were certainly a mixed bag, a few old sweats who had been on the squad perhaps longer than they should have been, some new kids who were certainly motivated, but lacked experience, and a couple of WDC's who gave me the impression that they weren't being taken seriously enough. I reassured the two women in no uncertain terms that they were important to me and to the squad, and that seemed to perk them up.

After seeing them all, I thought they seemed a bit more buoyant. I just had to wait and see how it all went over the next few days. The new operation would give me a chance to see how they worked together, but I did have reservations about one DC. His name was Mal Hopkins. Mal had about ten years' service and no obvious ambition. It was clear from his file that he got in to the job on the strength of his sporting prowess. He played semi-pro rugby before joining. However, a few years in, he picked up a serious knee injury, which finished his sport. I sighed when I scanned his postings. Rather than put him somewhere out of the way, some dozy bastard had decided to drop him on to the squad.

Hopkins worried me. He was built like a brick shithouse, over six feet tall, and had more muscle on his dick than I had on my whole body. To be honest, he looked like the love child of Arnold Schwarzenegger and Jocelyn Wildenstein. I could imagine him bursting through the front door with a rammer in his hands and screaming, *"I told you I'd be back, in a minute, mun."*

I had heard on the grapevine that he had also been a competitive body builder prior to joining the force and that he didn't get all his muscle down the gym. In fact, it was pretty bloody apparent to anyone who saw him that he was a 'juicer.' I didn't broach the subject with him during the one-to-one. I guessed it wouldn't be long before I got to know for sure if he was still doing a bit. I didn't want anyone like that on my squad. Juicers were totally unpredictable. Calm one minute and the next they're the Incredible Hulk. I knew I had to keep a sly eye on Mal Hopkins.

I sipped a shot of my whisky behind my closed office door and stared at Hopkins' photo. He had the classic juicer jaw, he had slitty eyes and puffed up lips. Seeing his mush made me think back to when I was a young bobby on the beat in Bridgend. We had a call during the early hours of a Sunday to the Benz nightclub on Tremain Road. Some bloke was off his face, smashing the place up. When we got there, this bloke was stripped to his waist, throwing tables, chairs, and just about anything else that came to hand. Nobody could get near him. He had practically emptied the club. There was glass everywhere, it was a mess. The inspector tried to talk to him and all he got for his trouble was a huge right-hander that sent him skidding across the dance floor.

The dog was called in. The dog had the unusual name of Robbie and I knew him of old and therefore used to give him a wide berth. Like most of his hairy colleagues, he'd bitten more coppers than villains. The dogs were great to have on your side and usually did the trick by barking the shits out of people. But this bloke just picked Robbie up by the shoulders as the dog snarled and gnashed his fearsome teeth at him and hurled Robbie across the room, like a canine rag doll. You had to be there to believe it. The bloke seemed possessed by some demon that liked to cut up rough whenever it could channel itself through some well-built, poor unsuspecting sap. So, in the end, we all had to pile in. It took about eight of us to rush him at the same time and to eventually subdue the bastard. Turned out he was a body builder from Swansea who'd been jacking himself up on the old 'roids. I'll never forget him. In my mind I had these visions of Hopkins turning nasty like that on my watch, not a pretty sight, I thought.

8

I had called the squad together to update them on the information gleaned from the airport operation. After giving them the nuts and bolts of what had occurred, I let Mike and Steve take the floor.

Steve began, "The two individuals have been identified as Raymond John Dean, born 11.8.1980. His home address is a house called Bogota in Bell-end Street..." he paused whilst the team laughed and he pretended he had trouble reading his notes. "Sorry... that's Bell Street, Barry. CRO number 499401, unemployed. Pre-cons for possession, actual bodily harm and taking a vehicle without consent of the owner. Dean is also the registered owner of the silver BMW. Divorced with two young kids aged eight and ten. He lives alone.

"The other bloke is Lawrence Smith, born 29.11.80. Home address is at a house called... wait for it... 'Escobar' in Castle Street, Barry. Bit of a cheeky twat, it seems. CRO number 131240, also unemployed. Pre-cons for burglary, deception and T.W.O.C. He's single and lives alone."

Mike chipped in, "Both are well known to local police, plenty of intelligence on them regarding involvement locally with drugs. Suspected of supplying, but neither have ever been nicked in possession. Been pulled a few times, but always clean."

"As you can see," Steve added, "both are unemployed but, by all accounts, they live the high life, always plenty of cash and their pads are done up to the nines. Now, unless they have a special arrangement with the DSS, I have to suspect that some other form of income supplements their finances. Doesn't take a genius to work out what that might be with these two fucking muppets. That's about it on Kermit the Frog and Fozzy Bear, like I say, plenty of intel, but nothing concrete. I'll let Mike fill you in on the bloke they met at the airport."

Mike nodded his thanks to Steve and sighed as he stretched his arms. "Well, ladies and gents, there's not a lot I can really say about Joost Van Gerber, only that he was born in Maastricht on the 1.8.1970. He's from a very privileged background. His father was a doctor, his mother an English teacher. At the moment, he runs his own business..." he checked his notes, "*Gerber Antiques* out of Maastricht. Not known to the Dutch police for any criminality, to all intents and purposes he's clean as a whistle. I've sent a request to the Met' Europol Liaison Officer for an update, but I don't hold out much hope for anything more. So, why is our Dutchman associating with these two scumbags from Barry? Neither look as if they're fans of The

Antiques Road Show, but I think they're more inclined to that other one... what's it called? 'Flog it!'" The joke wasn't lost on the team. The groans around the room made that clear. "And that's about it, boss," Mike added. "By the way," he said. "This little job is now called *Operation Hydra*."

Every operation had to have a codename. It was tradition and was steeped in history from a time long before I joined the service. It was based in the need for secrecy, but it was also easier to refer to a codename than to explain the guts of the operation – the aims and intentions – each time it was brought up. Operation Hydra seemed a bit over the top. Hydra had many heads but the only ones I knew of in this case were three, at present. Perhaps Mike expected many more to be exposed over the duration of the enquiry.

I then took the floor. "Right, ladies and gents, this is a new dawn for the squad and by the looks of it we're going to start with a cracker. Any suggestions?"

I had always liked to get the troops involved from the outset, not to appear too overbearing.

Colin Anderson, my other DS stood. "Simple, boss. Let's do a week of surveillance on the pair and see where it takes us."

I looked around at the faces of the assembled team. "Well, you heard what Colin has suggested, are you all up for it?"

They seemed to be chomping at the bit. I could see it in their eyes and body language. I began to think I had them all singing off the same hymn sheet and it hadn't been as painful as I had thought it would be. I'd have to remember to thank Joost and his pals for giving me something to boost the squad moral.

"Right then, Mike. We'll need observation points on their homes. I want you to arrange that. We'll have a couple of days static, just to see what their habits are, and then we'll go mobile."

"I take it you lot are all now trained up?" I said. "I don't want any cock ups on this one, I've got a good feeling about it.

"Who's my bike man?" I asked. A hand popped up. It was one of the female DC's, Jane Francis. "OK. Your role will be paramount in this operation. I want you down in Barry forthwith, cruising and getting to know the area. You know their vehicle and with the info, when it comes, you can give us a head start for when the full team is deployed in a few days' time. Book yourself into a B&B for a couple of nights."

"Thank you, boss," she smiled. "Leave it to me. Are we talking five-star accommodation?"

She was clearly keen as mustard and had a sense of humour, I liked that. "Five *scar* is more like it down that neck of the woods," I said.

I looked around the faces. "Right then, I want

an office manager, any volunteers?" There was a deathly hush and I thought I'd said something politically incorrect or something. "Come on," I said, "there must be one of you who doesn't want to be in a car all day and night with your mates farting and busting for a piss?"

A hand finally rose slowly into the air. "I'll do it, boss." DC Jeff Hyatt had a wealth of experience but was clearly carrying a bit of weight. He reminded me of an old dog on his last legs. I thought about it for a moment. Perhaps it was time for him to come in from the cold before he went off to the kennel in the sky.

"Thank you, Jeff," I said. "You'll be playing an important role in this operation, everything comes through you, all the intelligence, communications, the whole shooting match. You'll keep me up to speed with what's happening on the ground. So, if I ask you the state of play you better bloody know it."

He gave me a wry smile of approval. "No problem, boss. I'm happy to do that."

"Right. The rest of you make sure that all the vehicles are fit for purpose, radios encrypted, false plates all stored, change of clothing, you all know the drill.

"One last thing..." I said. "You tell no one about this Op.' No pillow talk, nothing. This is our baby. The Customs are unaware, as are the local boys.

The only others who are aware of this are the airport SB, and, as you know, they're spooks and don't tell anybody anything. Now, you can all clear off and do the business for me. I'll call a conference in a couple of days and hopefully we'll have more intel on this pair of bastards."

9

The gym was buzzing when DC Mal Hopkins entered and strolled through the vast array of odd shaped exercise machines. He had taken the first watch at the home of the drug dealers they were watching for Operation Hydra and at one point he wondered whether he'd get any time down at the gym. Thankfully, he had been stood down an hour ago and replaced by a colleague. Hopkins would be back on point in eight hours' time – a double back shift. Still, there was time for a workout before a few hours kip.

If any place could resemble a torture chamber, then this gym would be it. But Hopkins loved it. He loved the smell of sweat and stale aftershave, of liniment and the perfume of the girls who were also addicted to exercise. He also loved the sounds of metal crashing back from a rep and the grunts and groans of muscle fibres tearing as they began the normal process of repair and growth. But Hopkins didn't have time for the normal process of repair and growth. There were so many ways of speeding up the process and he had long ago found the ideal method for his body. He knew what he was doing was illegal and that he'd certainly lose his job if he was rumbled, but he also knew he was addicted to the benefits and didn't worry about any side effects that may one day take their toll. Tomorrow was another day and at least today he would look good. He believed that it was his addiction to the 'roids that made him understand the druggies better than any of his colleagues. It made him a better drug squad officer. It was just that the rest of the team didn't understand or appreciate that. They had no idea.

He stepped into the changing room and dropped his bag onto the wooden slats of the bench that occupied one wall of the narrow room. On the opposite wall, and within touching distance of the bench, was a line of tall metal lockers. Hopkins fished out his key and popped the padlock. He stripped his outdoor clothes from his ripped torso and admired himself in the mirror attached to the inside of his locker door. He pulled his training kit from the bag and dropped the empty holdall into the bottom of the locker and hung his clothes from the hangers attached to a bar suspended from the top.

It was chest and arms day. Hopkins made four visits to the gym every week and each day had a specific set of exercises that had to be completed. He secured the locker door and strolled out to the machine he favoured for his pecs.

He planned on ten reps of eight at two-thirds maximum weight, followed by a blast of two sets that would push him to the point of collapse. There was nothing quite like the buzz of a good workout, knowing that each rep was adding a fraction more growth to his frame. It was also great to see the young women sneaking a glance in his direction from time to time. He knew that they admired his physique. Anyone who trained regularly couldn't help but admire his physique. If Hercules had a brother, it would be Hopkins.

"Looking good," the voice from behind him said.

Hopkins didn't have to look around to know who was speaking; he didn't even break his rhythm.

"You OK for this week?" the voice said.

Hopkins dropped the bar back into the stand and sat up with a groan. "The usual?"

Phil Dawson tapped Hopkins on his bulbous shoulder. Hopkins growled. "Don't fucking touch me. You know the score."

"Hey! Just being friendly. No need to be a stroppy twat."

Dawson wasn't quite as big as Hopkins but he had a reputation for being mean. That meant nothing to Hopkins. He always fancied his chances against the bloke. He tolerated Dawson because he supplied him with what he wanted, what he needed, and at a tidy price. But Hopkins also knew that Dawson tolerated him because he was an important link in the chain, and it was always useful to have a copper involved. Never knew when he might come in handy.

Hopkins knew the day would come when the

bastard would 'cash him in' but he had made it pretty damn clear to Dawson that if he did it would cost him his life.

For the moment, they had a convivial relationship, but that didn't mean Dawson could touch him like a mate.

10

We didn't get a lot from the observation points. It looked as though both targets had wound down for a couple of days, no visitors, no comings and goings at their addresses.

I strolled around the team room and felt like a spare prick at a wedding, a chocolate fireguard, a glass hammer, then I couldn't think of another oxymoron and wondered if I'd been taken for a *proper* moron?

I slumped down in a chair near Jeff. What the hell was going on with our targets, what were they up to? I was now wondering if this was a load of old bollocks.

I finally made a decision. I needed some grub and left Jeff to carry on doing nothing.

After two days of observations, all we had was Dean picking up Smith in the Beemer, usually in the evenings, and then driving to the Highwayman Pub on Port Road.

In fairness to Jane, she kept tabs on them each time they visited, even kept an eye on them in the pub. It's a tough job but someone had to do it.

"Nothing out of the ordinary with them," she said, "played pool most of the time. No dealing or anything. One thing I did notice was that none of them drank alcohol, it was always soft drinks."

I thought that was unusual for two players like them, but then on the other hand, they probably didn't want to be pulled in by Traffic and bagged, either? They weren't quite as dull as they looked.

I called the team together again and decided that we would do a full seventy-two-hour surveillance on the targets on the weekend. It would be a blitz. By a full surveillance, I meant five cars and a bike, all plotted up around the addresses, together with observation points.

Mike would run the operation, with Steve and Colin out on the ground with the team.

It was going to take a lot of manpower and I would run it for the full seventy-two hours, starting at midday on the Friday. If this proved fruitless, then I was sunk.

Friday came and Mike sorted out the crews, all double manned and of course Jane on her 650 Yamaha. Fair play to her, she could certainly ride the bloody thing. She was like shit off a shovel – head down and arse up wherever she went on the thing.

As for me, I had a lot more occupying my mind. I couldn't forget the problems Karl faced, nor could I forget the money Coulter had accumulated – another bent copper I'd locked up – or the villainy carried out by Detective Chief Inspector Cliff Ambrose before he was finally brought to book. There was also Steve Diamond in prison on Dartmoor – when I promised him I'd get him closer to home – and the new problem I had on my watch with the Incredible Hulk. All in all, plenty to keep me occupied.

There wasn't much I could do about the diary, or Steve Diamond, but I knew I had to do something about Hopkins the Hulk. I had a mate in Professional Standards, a guy I'd worked with as a DC during my first few years of service, so I gave him a bell to see if he could fill me in on the Hulk, because if he'd been given the gipsy's warning about his steroid use by Cliff then there was obviously serious cause for concern. It must have been bad for Cliff to pull him in over it. Now that was a bright bastard to give a juicer appropriate advice.

Anyway, I spoke to my mate and he confirmed, the 'roid rumour and that the Hulk was now doing a bit of dealing around the local fitness centres, nothing concrete, all just rumours. Rumour or not, that was enough for me. I would play it by ear and see what I could glean from within the squad, I might even get a few training tips off him.

The more I thought about it and with my brain going twenty to the dozen, young PC Caroline Williams came to mind. She had been keen to get an aide on CID, but my promise to her had come to nothing thus far. My move from divisional CID to the drug squad had messed up that chance for her, but I wondered if I could use her in any way with the Hulk. It was just a thought. She might be up for it.

There was definitely a trip to the Moor on the agenda to see Diamond in relation to Coulter and to apologise for not sorting out his move. I made a note to myself to do something about Diamond as soon as this Op was over. Although Diamond was a convicted killer, he had been keen to supply me with information on Cliff Ambrose during that investigation, and seemed to know what was going on even though he was behind bars.

Both Cliff Ambrose and Chris Coulter – who had stitched up several small-time villains to make themselves look good – no longer had a pot to piss in. The courts had taken away all their assets, the whole shooting match, houses, cars and cash, everything. It made me smile. That'll teach the bent pair of bastards and nothing hurt a villain more than the loss of assets.

There was more to sort out in relation to Coulter. There was a little matter of over four-hundred grand that had been seized from him by the court and I wanted to know where it came from. It had nothing to do with me now, but Diamond was my contact and he seemed amenable to a chat if I could sort out a move closer to home for him. As a lifer, his incarceration so far from home would hurt his wife and kids more than him and, whilst it was his own fault he was there, I couldn't help feeling sorry for his family.

11

The team were deployed. I wished them well and told them to keep safe. I didn't have to be around because Mike was sound as a pound. No news would be good news when Mike was on the job. I always thought that if any of my officers rang me it meant they wanted me out to sort something for them. I often heard that other teams would just ring to let the chief know what was happening. That sort of thing always made me think that the caller was a bit inadequate. I liked officers who could make decisions on the hoof. If they dropped a ricket, so what? I was always on hand with the shit shovel to clear up the mess later.

As soon as the squad were deployed, I opened my top drawer and poured myself a small malt. Swivelling back in my chair, I wondered what Monday would bring? I finished my drink and bid Jeff Hyatt, my office manager, a good weekend. Actually, I just hoped he'd be able to keep awake. Seventy-two hours without kip is a long time. At least he wasn't going to be on his own. We had teamed him up with another two of the squad who were superfluous to the surveillance job.

As for myself? I thought I would spend a couple of quality days with Molly, whilst I had a chance. It had been a long time since we spent some time alone together. I didn't think anything worthy of an arrest would happen over the weekend. All I wanted was something, anything that would reveal their intentions. Perhaps they'd lead us to others in the chain. If we just ended up getting half a dozen extra names that might be connected then it would have at least not been a failure.

***

I think Molly was a bit shocked to see me home so early. I remembered a time shortly after we got married, when I was a young DC on division. Molly had cooked a fabulous Sunday lunch. I was on my way home when I got lumbered with a nasty section 18 wounding, who'd have thought, a stabbing at lunchtime on a Sunday? They were usually to be expected late on a Saturday night but not when I had a lovely dinner waiting for me at home. That messed up our lunch and any idea Molly might have had that our life together would be normal.

The only time Molly would cook for me now was if I was physically present, in the house, within spitting distance of the dining table, and that was as rare as a good hair day for Donald Trump.

I worshipped my Molly. She had been my rock throughout most of my service. She knew and accepted the life of being married to a man who spent more time in work than at home with her. She accepted that the work I did was important, and she accepted that things would not change until the day

I retired. But she also accepted my promise to her that I would never cheat on her and would never want for anyone other than her. I would go to the ends of the earth for her. God help any bastard who tried to hurt or take advantage of her. I just couldn't think what I would do if something happened to Molly. It was the one thing that I knew would destroy me.

Molly had really gone to town with setting the scene for dinner. She loved to get the *ambiance* right, she had once told me. She had the obligatory candles scattered around the dining room and must have added an extra couple of degrees to the Global Warming data. She cooked me a steak and absolutely nailed it. It didn't need a knife to cut it and the homemade pepper sauce could have been bottled and would easily have rivalled anything that Paul Newman could have thrown together.

We had a lovely, relaxing evening, a nice bottle of Sauvignon Blanc, or was it two? It was bliss. It was just like the nights we had when we were courting, and my work hours were regular and she could depend on my time keeping. How times changed.

On the Saturday, we drove up to the Brecon Beacons and did a bit of walking in scenery that I have always believed is amongst the most spectacular anywhere in the world. We scaled the highest peak, something I had done many times in the past but it was a first for Molly.

After we'd done enough walking and talking, we stopped off for a pub lunch and talked some more over a ploughman's and a pint. I made a point of not mentioning anything of my job and Molly was clearly happy with that. We laughed, hugged and kissed and re-discovered feelings that we thought had been lost with time and far too much space between us. I caught myself staring at her across the bar table and wondering how I had managed to win the heart of such a special woman. I also caught myself before I said as much. I have never been good at voicing my feelings for her, but I knew she knew and that was something. One day I'd tell her and I was sure that when that day came, she'd have the biggest shock of her life.

We drove home as the sun was setting and relaxed in front of the fire with another glass or two of the white. It was my idea of heaven and I caught myself thinking that perhaps I would be better off in uniform. At least the hours would be regular. Perhaps the ACC could fix me up with a cushy little posting, nine-to-five, regular, with weekends off. Then I came down to earth. It sounded good, but I knew the regular work would do my head in.

Sunday was also a bit special. Molly made us a roast Welsh lamb dinner with all the trimmings. I told her she should enter MasterChef. We sat and cleared every last morsel from our plates. Molly looked across the table at me and smiled sadly. "I bet this will be the last time we have a weekend like this for a while."

Molly knew me too well. I couldn't get away with much, but she knew that my job meant so much to me. She really was my rock. That weekend was just what we both needed, but I knew that if things with the new operation went according to plan, family time would be at a premium soon.

12

I got into the office early on Monday morning. Jeff was sitting with his feet up on a desk, ogling the third page of some daily rag and sipping a mug of coffee.

"Morning, boss. All quiet!" he said. "In fact, it's been much the same all weekend, not a lot of movement down in Barry."

"Cheers, Jeff. Thanks a bunch," I groaned. "Get me a coffee, mate? Make it strong and black. I think the wheels might have come off this one, butt."

I slumped in my high-back chair and sank into the buttoned leather cushions; hands cupped the back of my head, deep in thought. The files from my old office that had been troubling me for last couple of months were now in cardboard boxes on the floor of my new office. I would have to sort them out. I'd probably end up taking them from the boxes and piling them on the floor just as before.

I was disappointed that nothing of value had happened over the weekend. What were those two bastards up to? No dodgy pair of druggies meets a Dutch businessman for no reason. There had to be more to it. I had that feeling in my gut. I had heard it said many times before that all coppers have got a sixth sense, but I knew that was a bit of a fallacy. Only the thinkers and the doers possessed that feeling. The others just pretended that they did.

At midday, Mike rolled into the main office with the team. They look knackered and I could understand that. Surveillance was no picnic; sitting on your arse for hours on end, especially when there was nothing going on to keep you interested. I was expecting the worse, so I let Mike have the floor.

"Well, boss," he began. "This pair of arseholes never did a lot over the weekend. I would go as far to say they might have the heads up on us. Saw nothing out of the ordinary, it was either the Highwayman pub or each other's house."

I cut in. "Oh great, Mike. As Clint says, 'make my day.'"

Mike then began to grin. "There's a little more to add..."

"Go on," I said.

"They did go to one place which I thought was a bit odd."

"Carry on," I said, getting a little more impatient.

"At about 4 a.m. on Sunday morning, they made their way to a storage unit at Verlon Close, on the Verlon Industrial Estate in Barry. It's not a big unit, it probably could house a couple of Transit type vans at a push. Roller shutter doors, no windows and detached from any other units."

"Very interesting," I said. "What did they do when they got there?"

Mike shrugged. "Nothing, they just opened up and spent about half an hour inside. Didn't take anything in or bring anything out."

"Any chance of an obs point nearby?"

"No, but the surveillance van wouldn't be out of place there. We'd have a terrific front-on view of the roller doors."

I grimaced as I took a sip of the coffee Mike had made for me. "Well that's something, I suppose. There's got to be something going on... any other suggestions?"

One of the younger lads, DC Simon Church spoke up. "I used to be stationed in Barry, know it like the back of my hand," he said, "still got a few narks down there. I could put the feelers out. I'm still owed a few favours, you never know?"

"You carry on, Churchy. See what you can come up with," I said. "We need something pretty quick because if there's anything going down with the Dutchman, it will happen pretty soon. Get down there, you'll have until Wednesday morning..." I waited for some action, but my team seemed just as bothered at the lack of good info as I was. "Well? What are you waiting for?"

They began to drag themselves up from their chairs, but I held up my hand. "Have a few hours' kip first."

They all looked relieved. "The same goes for the rest of you," I said to the office staff. "Get home, freshen up and have a good night's sleep, see you all in the morning."

I asked Mike and Churchy to stay behind for a few minutes.

Churchy looked worried, for some reason. "What's up, boss?" he asked.

"I've got a very important job for you, before you head for some kip. You up for it?"

He looked unsure but nodded his head.

I handed him the mug of coffee Mike had made for me. "Throw that mug of shit down the drain and teach Mike how to make a decent cup of coffee and then head off home."

Churchy laughed.

"What's wrong with my coffee?" Mike moaned.

"Nothing, if you want to strip paint off your walls."

I knew that Mike would have gleaned plenty of information out of the team over a seventy-two-hour period and would have a better picture of the squad mood and any personality clashes.

He waited for Churchy to disappear after the lad had made two fine cups of coffee. Even Mike agreed it was better than his shit.

"The general consensus was that Cliff was a waste of space," he said. "He had no interest at all, just delegated. He was very rarely in the office and left the squad to their own devices."

I could understand that.

"Any personality clashes, Mike?"

He looked around to make sure Simon

'Churchy' Church had left. "Only the one," he whispered, "between Hopkins and Churchy."

"That would be a mismatch," I observed. Churchy was half the size of the Hulk and looked like one of the druggies he dealt with. "What's that all about?"

Mike shrugged. "Well, Churchy doesn't rate him. Mind you, he's not the only one. They went toe-to-toe a few months back in the office. As big as the Hulk is, Churchy gave as good as he got."

That really did surprise me.

"Apparently, Hopkins took the piss out of Churchy for being a skinny twat and Churchy then made some smart-arse comment that he could be big too if he was on 'roids and pretty much said out loud that Hopkins was still juicing. To be honest, Terry, I've had Hopkins all weekend and his moods have been up and down like a fucking yo-yo. If it isn't the steroids, it's something else."

I slurped some more of the good coffee and weighed up the implications. If I did nothing, then it would probably get worse and if it went tits up and the Hulk got caught we'd all be in the shit for doing nothing about it. If I pulled him in, tested him and booted him out, that might cause some issues for the others in the team.

"I think we should have him tested," Mike said, as if he was reading my mind.

"No, we'll do better than that," I said. "We'll bust him. I've got something mapped out for the

Hulk. Take Churchy one side and find out what gym the Hulk uses, get it on the QT. Tell Churchy there'll be no comeback on him. Now you head off and have some kip as well."

I could see Mike was concerned by my plan, but I also knew he'd back me all the way.

I stayed in the office until about 8 o'clock and then rang Molly to tell her I was on my way.

I arrived home just after nine and I cracked open a can of Guinness and Molly did me some scrambled eggs on toast and, boy, did I need it? I was so wrapped up in my own thoughts that I almost missed the fact that Molly was a bit subdued and not her usual self.

I gave her a cwtsh and whispered in her ear, "You OK, love?"

Then she began to cry. This was not like Molly. Molly never cried without good reason. I sat her down on the settee and hugged her. "What's wrong, Mol? Is it the kids?"

She shook her head.

"Is it the hours I'm working again? It won't be for too long..."

She shook her head again and I could feel her nails dig into my arm.

I gently pushed her head away to look her in the eyes. Something bad had happened. "Is it the kids?" I said again. I couldn't think of anything else that could... then I thought she might have found something like a lump and my heart sank.

She shook her head.

"Then what is it, Molly? Please... you're worrying me... are you ill?"

She stifled a sob and took a deep breath. "Some bloke rang here earlier. He said he'd burn the house down with us both in it... that it would happen soon."

"What? Who was it?" I was relieved Molly and the kids were alright but I was tamping mad that someone had the nerve to ring my home and threaten my wife. Molly shook her head and shrugged her shoulders. I checked the last number that had called in to our phone and it was showing up as 'number withheld.'

"Did he ask for me?"

"No, that was all he said."

I wiped the tears from her eyes. "Probably some random twat I must have had a run-in with at some time or other. Don't worry about it, try and forget about it."

I could see Molly wasn't convinced and that I was going to have to spend a lot more time persuading her to let it go and that everything would be fine.

I had that gut feeling again. Our home telephone number was withheld and nobody should know it, other than close friends and family. I thought of that crooked bastard Cliff Ambrose, and wondered if he'd got hold of some low-life bastard to put the frighteners on us from inside the nick. Cliff had my number, we were friends once, but after I'd locked the arsehole up it hadn't occurred to me to change the telephone number. Stupid!

My blood was boiling and at that moment in time, I swore to myself that I would find out who it was and then the shit would hit the fan for them. Nobody would hurt Molly or any of the kids. For the first time since the kids had grown up and left home, I was actually glad they weren't at home anymore. I also began to wonder if they were safe? They were both on opposite sides of the globe to us and I doubted anyone would be able to find them. Certainly not anyone Cliff could now afford to hire.

All my years of dealing with the scum of the earth, I'd never had a problem until now. It had to be Cliff. Who else could it be? It's true that I had lots of people who would want to give me a kicking for locking them up, some would also probably like to make that kicking a bit more severe, but there were few around who would actually try to top a copper. Killing a police officer was a one-way ticket to a very long sentence.

We sat together and watched a bit of telly until about 11pm and then went to bed. I gave Molly a kiss and we spooned up close until we both finally drifted off to sleep.

***

I swear that my head hadn't been on the pillow for more than ten minutes when the phone rang. If it was one of those PPI cold-callers, they were in for a right mouthful of abuse, then I realised that even those parasites wouldn't ring at that time of night.

"Hello. Terry McGuire…"

"Boss. It's Churchy. You're right, they're at it big time. My nark says they're smuggling booze and drugs in via France. They've got two lemons from Barry doing the runs for them and so far, everything is going well."

I wanted to say, 'Well, fuck off and tell me in the morning,' but what I actually said was, "Well done, Churchy. Can you fix it for me to meet the nark? I want to hear it first hand and sort the finances with him. Do you think he'll be up for it?"

"No problem, boss. I'll sort it and speak with you in the morning."

"Well done, Churchy. See you in the morning."

Even after having my precious sleep disturbed and the telephone threats, my life seemed a little bit better after that call. The loss of fathers, mothers, sisters, brothers, daughters and sons, all dying from using drugs, strikes at my soul. Anything I could do to stop the evil trade had a tendency to make me feel just a little bit better. My head hit the pillow for a second time, and I went out like a light.

13

Caroline Williams sat patiently inside the unmarked car, waiting for the call. She checked her notes. If the bloke kept to the pattern she had recognised, then he would appear any time in the next hour.

The flasher had become known as the 'Dick of the Dunes' within the station. Many of her uniform colleagues thought it was just a petty enquiry, but Caroline had a building sense of dread. The flasher had exposed himself seven times over the past three months and as the weeks slipped towards the holiday season she knew she had to catch him before visitor numbers grew. Caravan holidays in Trecco Bay drew families with children and the last thing the resort needed was a nutter running around bollock naked.

The pattern suggested the flasher was a creature of habit. He seemed to favour a Tuesday or a Sunday between 6 and 9 in the morning. There had been one incident where the flasher had done the business at 7 pm on a Friday evening but that was the only occasion. He seemed to prefer the morning for some odd reason. Caroline's colleagues suggested he must suffer from the dawn-horn.

A lot depended on Caroline catching the flasher. She had been promised an aide on the local CID, but that had fallen flat after DI Terry McGuire had been promoted to Chief Inspector and moved to the drugs squad. He had made a deal with her. Catch the flasher and the aide was hers. The aide might well have fallen by the wayside, but she was still determined to prove to herself that she could do the business and bring the pervert to justice.

She checked her watch and the messages on her phone. A text had just appeared asking her to contact DCI McGuire at the drug squad at her earliest convenience. She smiled. Perhaps he was keeping to his word. Whatever. It didn't change the fact that she knew she had to stop the flasher. If it escalated further there would be shit flying everywhere. The local newspaper had already run a short piece on the case and that would definitely expand to criticism of the force if it got worse and she would be the focus of that criticism. With only just over three years in the job, she certainly didn't want to blot her copybook.

She checked the rest of the texts. Nothing. She had enlisted the help of some local residents; an old gent and one of the women who had seen the flasher. They had agreed to send a text to her if they saw the Dick of the Dunes. They were ideally placed on the site, each having a caravan in areas that had been targeted by the pervert.

She checked the charge on her phone. She didn't want it to run out on her before the end of her observations. With just a quarter of the charge remaining, she plugged her charger lead into the cigarette lighter port and started the engine just as her phone pinged with a new message:

Flash is behind C62 on front row of vans now! Emma.

Caroline put the car in gear and drove a hundred metres towards the line of caravans that used the 'C' prefix as an address identifier. C62 was on the far end of the line but she knew the flasher would hear the car engine if she approached any closer. She tugged her phone from the charger and locked the car door. She sent a smiley emoticon to her shift sergeant – the prearranged signal he would recognise as a silent call for backup.

She checked for her cuffs and extendable baton that she had brought from the station, in case the flasher cut up rough. She tucked them all under her civilian coat and slipped her phone into the back pocket of her jeans. Satisfied, she began jogging towards the location sent to her via the text.

She stopped short of the target caravan and began to walk, trying to appear to any onlookers as a holidaymaker simply out for a stroll.

14

I met Churchy, as arranged, in the office. He was like a dog on heat and the whole office had a real buzz, something that had been missing when I first met the squad.

It was obvious that Churchy had told them about the nark, I didn't see anything wrong with that, but I had to speak to the guy on my own.

I could tell by the faces of the others that they didn't mind this at all. However, I did notice that the Hulk seemed a bit odd, somewhat sombre, and was hardly making eye contact with anyone. I couldn't understand why the big twat wasn't over the moon. Well, this was going to be the last operation with him. He had to go, one way or another.

Churchy followed me into the office with Mike.

"OK, just lay it on me," I said.

Churchy shrugged. "Well, boss, my nark is a bloke by the name of Gavin Marshall. He's got a bit of form, mostly for assault, the last time I had dealings with him I put him away for a three stretch for GBH."

"And how is he so amenable towards you now?"

Churchy looked between Mike and me as if we should already know the answer. When I stood with my arms crossed and my gob shut, he finally caught on. "Oh, eh, when Marshall was away in the pokey I looked after his bird and his two kids..." he could see from my raised eyebrows that I required a more detailed explanation.

"No, boss, not like that, not in the... howdy-do-dee sense... I mean, I sorted out their benefits and had them rehoused until he was released. He's never forgotten that."

"And why would you do that, exactly? You some kind of soft twat or something?"

Churchy looked shocked. "No, boss. I just thought he'd be grateful. I didn't have a nark at the time, and I thought it was a good way to get one."

"Very enterprising of you," I said, sarcastically. I'd never done that sort of thing myself. I knew only too well that many coppers played at 'being kind' just to get favours in return. I never had to work like that, and I was not going to start this late in my career – although I had done deals for narks after the event. Diamond was an example. Good turns inevitably brought favours as payback but there were other ways I preferred to do it.

"Is he reliable, Churchy?" I asked the eager puppy.

Churchy shrugged. "I reckon so, boss. He didn't need any prompting, in fact he said that Dean and Smith believe they are a bit untouchable and he thinks they may be getting their 'heads up' from within."

"I hope you don't mean the drug squad?" I said, suddenly feeling a deep dread once more. "I thought I'd put all that nonsense to bed with Cliff?"

"No, boss. This sounds more like a uniform source."

That didn't make me feel any better. "So, what did he say, in a nutshell?

"Well, there are two young lemons from Barry, who Dean and Smith have been using as gophers to do liquor and ciggie runs from France. They drive over in a white Transit van, meet their contacts, do the business and return. My nark says they're also collecting the drugs and think booze and ciggies will distract the Customs from what they're really into. They probably don't mind losing the booze and things as long as the Customs don't find the real gear. They're making a good living out of it."

Made sense to me. "I think it's time I met Mr Marshall. Have you sorted a time and place?"

"Yes, his parents have got a caravan down in the Fontygary Park. He's given me the number and I told him we'd pop along at midday."

"Do we know the two lemons?"

"Oh aye. Brandon Wilson and Logan Bennett.

"They sound like members of that poxy band, One Direction," I grinned. "Right, Mike, task Jeff with their antecedents, you know what I want, chapter and verse."

I thought it looked like it was all coming together nicely. I felt good.

"Right, Churchy my boy, let's get cracking."

Before leaving, I brought the squad up to speed whilst still keeping a beady eye on the Hulk. He still wasn't looking too happy. He had that vacant look of confused rage on his face – as if he knew he should be angry but didn't know why. I'd soon be putting an end to that. He was beginning to try my patience.

***

Fontygary Caravan Park was a place I'd passed many times before but never had occasion to visit. As a kid I'd spent many a holiday in Porthcawl's Sandy and Trecco bays but Fontygary was never on my list of dream destinations. On reflection, neither were Sandy or Trecco, but they were all my parents could afford at the time. Fontygary was only a stone's throw from Cardiff Airport and was nicely placed on prime land overlooking Fontygary Bay and the Bristol Channel.

We arrived there at 12:15pm. I never like being late for anything but didn't think Churchy's nark would be that bothered.

We finally met Gavin Marshall, as arranged. He shook my hand and offered us a cup of coffee. The caravan was spotless, so I didn't refuse. First rule of coppering – never accept a cup of anything from anyone until you've checked out the state of the kitchen.

I asked Marshall to go over the info that he'd

given to Churchy and, fair play, it was practically word for word. I had a few of my own questions, the first being, "What's in it for you, Gavin?"

He looked unfazed. "Listen, sir..."

I held up my hand. "Call me Terry."

He nodded and smiled politely. "Listen, Terry, Churchy put me away for a three stretch. But he put a good word in for me when I was sentenced, otherwise I would have had another two on top. He looked after my family, got them rehoused and made sure they had money to live on whilst I was in the slammer. I owe him big time, but as for those fuckers, Dean and Smith and Brandon and Logan? They can all go and kiss my hairy arse. Dean and Smith are punting around in a top of the range Beemer, flashing pots of money, whilst the likes of me scrimp and fucking scrape. Brandon and Logan are just as bad since they've been doing the runs. Pair of upwardly mobile twats. Is that a good enough reason for you?"

"That's good enough for me, Gav," I said. "Just a couple of things I'd like to ask you to do for me too... can you get the van registration number, the location where they store the gear, and most important, when the next run is?"

He pondered the question for a second and I began to think he was getting cold feet – all mouth and no balls – but then he came through for me. "I'll try my best," he said. "Should be able to. Brandon and Logan are always pissed or high, leave it to me, I've got Churchy's mobile, I'll give him a bell as soon as I have something."

I was impressed. Believe me, it took a special kind of arse-wipe villain to impress me. I was beginning to like Gavin. "Let me tell you something, Gav. If this works out, I'll make sure that there'll be more than a few quid for you as my way of saying thanks."

I watched his face and his reaction seemed genuine. He was almost overcome. I could only imagine that things must have been hard for him and his family and I began to regret thinking of him as an arse-wipe villain. He took a sharp intake of breath, looked at Churchy and said, "Churchy, is he real or what?"

I smiled. I began to understand where he was coming from. We all shook hands, I wished him and the family all the best and then left.

Result!

15

I didn't arrive in the office the following day until about ten. It was like the Marie Celeste, only quieter. Mike had got all the squad doing a bit of surveillance training, 'honing their skills,' I think they liked to call it. From what I'd seen, they needed more than just honing. As usual, Mike was leading from the front.

My mobile rang and it was Churchy.

"Boss, I got the info we want. It's a white Transit, registration number NC 62 FDZ and they'll be sailing from Dover at twelve-fifteen Saturday and returning the same day. The nark told me that he'd met the two of them in a local boozer last night and they just couldn't help themselves. Shot their mouths off like Janet Street-Porter."

"Well done, Churchy. Now tell the squad to get their arses back here a bit sharpish."

Within the hour, they were all back and I filled them in on what the nark had provided us and laid out the plan of attack.

Jane was dressed in her motorcycle leathers and had obviously been taking inappropriate comments from the lads. She was clearly used to it and sat with a smug grin on her face and the single digit of her right hand extended in a permanent gesture for the benefit of the lads.

"Right then, Jane," I said, and chuckled as she realised her finger was still extended as I addressed her.

"Sorry, boss," she blushed.

"I want you and one car down to Barry first thing in the morning," I continued. "You keep obs on the white Transit van and the Beemer and you both then do the follow over to Calais on Saturday, if that's where they're going. Keep us updated all the way."

I turned to Mike. "We've got the obs van in place, so that's covered. Also, get the boys back in the OP's later on tonight to keep an eye on Dean and Smith. I want the five cars ready to be out on Saturday, double-crewed, and I'll arrange for a firearms officer in each car. We'll have a drugs dog on standby and also a few Traffic cars in the area for the next few days, in case they bring it all forward. I'll sort this with the ACC and there'll be a full briefing at ten in the morning with all officers concerned."

I left the team to sort things out and made my way over to see the ACC in headquarters. I knew from experience that as long as he wasn't busy with some admin nonsense, I'd have easy access to him. I asked his secretary if he was free and she gave him a bell. I could hear him telling her to send me in.

"How are you doing, Terry? Must be important?"

"It is, boss. We've got an operation on going.

It's a crowd from Barry bringing dope in from France."

"How big?"

"Hard to tell, but the initial info is that it could be very big. We've received good intel that a run is planned for Saturday."

The ACC smiled. He was a canny bastard and nothing much slipped past him. "Operation Hydra, I do believe?"

I smiled too.

"You've obviously settled in quick, Terry," he added, "It's been a while since the drug squad knocked on my door with a 'goer.' I take it you want firearms authorisation?"

The ACC Crime was as sharp as they came. He was born and bred in Toxteth, and I could see that he'd got Mystic Meg's DNA.

"I sure would, boss."

"No problem, Terry, you've got it."

I really liked him. He knew only too well that firearms authorisation was not something that could be taken lightly but I felt good that he trusted me, he took me on my word that they were needed. That's what I called *a boss*.

I then saw a grimace on his face and wondered what was coming?

"Customs and Excise involved, Terry?"

Before I could open my mouth, he sighed, "Obviously not."

"Terry, I have every confidence in you and, like

I told you when you took the job, you have a free hand. You have integrity... that's my way of saying that I have no reason to believe you'd fuck up. Do what you see fit."

I was lost for words and more than just a little embarrassed.

"What time's the briefing?"

"Ten tomorrow morning, boss."

He pondered the information for a moment. Then he nodded. "I'll be there, but don't tell the squad. I just want to see how they react. I won't be in uniform; I'll just blend in."

I laughed. As if he'd blend in.

"Thank you, Terry, but I must run. The Police and Crime Commissioner doth wait and I must endure another few hours of total bollocks. See you in the morning."

I left him to it. If only we had more like him. I pictured him as a Jack Russell terrier and most of the rest of the senior officers as butterflies or snakes.

16

Myself, Mike, Steve and Colin got in to the office a few minutes either side of 6 a.m. and we started planning the way forward for the operation. I felt it necessary to get in before the others to give us a few hours before the office became jam-packed with sweaty bodies.

I had Jeff on the communications, and he was ensuring all was OK at his end because all messages would be relayed through him. It was vital we didn't have any failures.

Jane and the lads had already called me and assured me that they were all in position and that the Transit was still parked outside Wilson and Bennett's home and hadn't moved all night. She was sure because she had made a passing note of the position of the air-filler caps on its wheels. The wheels couldn't possibly have moved.

The boys in the observation points had called in to say that the Beemer hadn't moved overnight either, for the same reason.

Well, I thought, that's a starter for ten. Normally, these types of blokes were always on the move, but were Dean and Smith normal? Perhaps they went somewhere on foot during the night whilst the team were resting. We just had to wait and see.

About half hour later, the rest of the squad drifted into the office and were followed ten minutes later by five armed-response boys, two dog handlers and two Traffic PC's to join the briefing.

By 9:45, the whole of the operational team, excluding those on point, had arrived. It was going to be a special day for the squad.

I introduced myself. "For those who don't know me, I'm Detective Chief Inspector Terry McGuire and this is DI Mike Johnston and DS's Colin Anderson and Steve Thompson," my team nodded and briefly acknowledged each other. "For your information, the operation has already begun," I let that sink in for a second or two. "I'll hand you over to Mike who's prepared packages for each of you. They contain all the relative information on the targets and your roles, but you'll have to wait for the release of those vital pieces of information. The packages will be issued to you on the day of the operation, which, as it stands, will be this Saturday."

Then, without fanfare, the ACC walked in. He was dressed casually, as if he was off to play a round of golf. Everyone in the room turned and immediately stood to attention. The ACC wanted none of the official nonsense and waved for them to sit down as he spoke. "I'm quite at home in the back here. Carry on, Mike," he said apologetically.

Mike composed himself and then laid out a brief overview of the forthcoming operation. It's never easy to give a briefing with the number two of the entire force standing at the back, especially one who had a background in detective work.

"The information we've received is that two villains from Barry are importing liquor and drugs into the area from Calais via Dover. Another pair of chancers and associates are the couriers.

"They have access to a silver Beemer and a white Transit, which they use to transport the goods. All reg numbers, and up to date photos of all targets are in the packages. You'll have little time to familiarise yourselves with all the information, but it's essential you are thorough," Mike warned. "We believe that the goods will be transported to a unit in Verlon Close in the Ty Verlon Industrial Estate, Cardiff Road, Barry. We should have eyes on it by now with the surveillance van and, should things come to fruition, they will give the order to strike... but we expect this to be on Saturday."

We discussed the requirements of the roles for each team and there was little else we wanted to divulge at that time. By keeping things tight within the squad, we would know the origins of any leak, should any occur. The rest of the team would have the packages a few hours before we went 'live' on Saturday.

The ACC saw his cue and walked towards me, turned towards the troops and shrugged. "I can't add anything to what has already been said. All I *will* say is, do the job to the best of your ability and keep safe, that's paramount."

He thanked all the officers, turned to me and took me aside. "If I don't hear from you, Terry, I'll assume that Hydra is a success and you can bring me up to speed first thing Monday morning."

***

The rest of the week passed without much incident. We had one or two false starts when the Transit drove from the house on Friday night. It turned out that one of the scrotes wanted to fill it up with diesel. It looked like they were getting ready to go.

Surveillance work seems glamorous when seen in films and on the telly, but the reality is far removed from any sort of glamour. Crews could spend days or weeks on point and sometimes without much to eat or drink. Conditions were never ideal, except that is when crews had to travel abroad on a tail and the rare occasion when the job ends whilst they're out there. Happened to me once, as a DC. I ended up following a suspected dealer from Bridgend to the south of France. When we got down there the bastard had a heart attack and snuffed it. We had to spend a couple of days liaising with the local Gendarmerie and I have to admit that they did look after us pretty well. But those jobs were extremely rare. This one was going to be a full day of travelling for the crew and then a rewarding bust if everything went to plan.

***

Saturday arrived and an early start was becoming the norm. I'd called for a couple of pints of milk to supplement the tea kitty and I was looking forward to the events of the day, whilst still nervous. So much could go wrong.

I called the meeting to order and then delegated. "I'll hand you over now to Colin and Steve. They'll be in control of the operation on the ground," I said.

Colin got the Hulk to pass the packages of information out to all the team and I watched him carefully and I still hadn't changed my mind. After this job, his arse wouldn't touch the ground.

Mike sat alongside me and Colin took the floor. "Ladies and gents, if you open your packages, you'll see that the targets are Raymond John Dean and Lawrence Charles Smith who we expect to be in the Beemer and Brandon Wilson and Logan Bennett who will be in the van. All the plotting positions around the estate are also listed. There'll be five double-crewed cars, each accompanied by an armed response officer. Call signs Alpha 1 to Alpha 5. The follow-car will be Alpha 6 and Jane and her bike will be Alpha 7.

"We have two dog handlers, one with the drug dog and one with the old German shepherd. Should anyone decide to run, their call signs are Kilo-one and Kilo-two.

"Last but not least, we have two Traffic cars..." Colin chuckled as some of the detectives jeered and booed. The Traffic lads laughed along. There was a long-standing friendly rivalry between departments but when the chips were down, they would always pull together. Well, nearly always. "Traffic will be in the vicinity on standby," Colin continued. "Should any chase ensue, use call signs Tango-Mike-one and Tango-Mike-two.

"All our vehicles will be car-to-car communication. However, try to keep the air as clear as possible. If things go to plan and arrests are made, all prisoners will be taken to the Bridgend Bridewell. None of them are to be taken to Barry. I repeat, none of them to Barry.

"All property is to be photographed in situ and the vehicles brought into HQ for examination by SOCO.

"Any questions, ladies and gents? Is everyone happy with their role?"

Colin waited a few moments, allowing a little thinking and reading time for the teams, and sipped from a can of energy drink. "I understand that the majority of you know each other one way or another, so that's a cracking start."

I stood. "Good luck to all of you. Keep safe and please don't take any chances. We're leaving it to you. Mike and I will be here monitoring the operation and if there are any problems you get in touch with us immediately.

"Hopefully, we'll have a good result. Remember, this is all about teamwork; everyone in this room will be playing an important part. Just one thing more... if the strike goes to plan and there are no chases, I want the two Traffic cars to make their way to the unit and assist if needed. Thank you all. So now please fuck off and do the business."

My statement was greeted with loud laughter and chuckling and even the Hulk smiled.

No sooner than my arse hit my chair, Jane rang, she sounded excited. "Wilson and Bennett are on the move in the van, boss. We're following."

"Carry on as briefed and keep us all updated as and when necessary."

"Will do, boss. Leave it with us," she had an air of confidence in her voice, I could tell she was enjoying it.

Jeff brought me a cup of black coffee. "Where's the milk?" I said.

"All those hairy-arsed bastards used it all during the briefing."

Now we had to wait without coffee? I didn't think so. I dug a quid out of my pocket and gave Jeff the task of getting some more. For me, long jobs revolve around coffee. With all the recent commercialisation of police services, I wondered if one day we'd be sponsored by Nescafé?

An hour passed with occasional updates from the follow-team. But I'd heard nothing for over thirty minutes. I paced the room, thinking out loud,

"Should have had an update by now."

Then the radio speaker, connected to the secure network monitoring the surveillance team, buzzed into life. The voice of Jane could be heard clearly around the room. "Targets are on the M4, they're over the bridge heading south-east."

Mike smiled. "She must be psychic,"

The others laughed.

"As you just heard the van is being followed down to Dover, so we have plenty of time to get plotted up before they return," Mike added.

17

She could hear the flasher moving at the far end of the long caravan. She could hear his booted feet crunch on the narrow strip of decorative gravel that the owner had set within a border around the raised wooden decking. Caroline had a feeling she was being stalked, a deer in the sights of the spoilt offspring of a multi-millionaire. She knew the flasher had seen her but assumed he still thought she hadn't seen him.

This was the second time in a week that she had been called to the park. The last time ended in disappointment. She had got to caravan C60 to find the informant and nothing else. The flasher had taken off as soon as he had heard Caroline's car. This time, Caroline had parked the car in the car park at the park reception, far away from the reported sighting.

She had walked the short distance to caravan F32, a van several lines back from the one she had been called to earlier in the week and crept as silently as possible between lines of mobile homes that were mainly still empty.

Now she was within striking distance. He was there and all she had to do was play it cool.

She took a deep breath and stepped along the side of the caravan towards the edge of the grass bank that then descended to the beach.

She reached the edge and stood still, pretending to admire the view. She could feel the flasher's presence behind her. Then she heard him. The bastard was groaning.

Turning and pretending to be surprised, Caroline saw the flasher now standing at the other end of the caravan, about fifteen metres away from her, and she could clearly see what he was doing.

Caroline feigned shock and horror and stepped slowly towards him. She could see him step back with each step she took. She tried to focus on his facial features but there was something odd about them. His face seemed familiar, yet somehow false. She couldn't quite work out what was wrong. She knew she had to do something to stop him. She looked around her, hoping the support was somewhere near but knew there hadn't been enough time. She had to delay him somehow.

"Why stand so far away?" she said in an alluring voice that was far removed from how she was feeling inside.

The flasher stopped what he was doing but his facial expression didn't change. It seemed fixed. *Odd.*

"I've got a caravan nearby. Why don't we go and spend a little time together?"

The flasher recommenced what he had been doing with his right hand and she noticed he held a paper tissue in his left. *No prizes for guessing what that was for.*

She took another step forward and smiled. She knew she would have to rush him or risk losing him amongst the hundreds of caravans on the site.

She heard the flasher groan, but his expression didn't change. Then he took off away from her at speed.

Caroline set off after him. "Stop!" she shouted but never expected him to heed the order. She was aware of the ridiculousness of the situation. He was only wearing boots and the sight of his lily-white arse-cheeks would have made her laugh under different circumstances.

The flasher ran across a narrow road and between a line of caravans. He was pulling away from Caroline as he ducked left. She was weighed down by the kit she was carrying and by the time she reached the end of the caravan he had gone from sight.

"Shit!" she gasped. She leaned against the caravan and noticed something near her feet. It was a crumpled white tissue.

Had the flasher made his first cock-up?

18

Caroline sat at the computer terminal, trawling through photographs of sex offenders known to be living in the force area.

She had bagged the tissue and sent it off for analysis and was disappointed to discover it could take up to a week for a result. Her case wasn't considered a high priority as far as the lab was concerned. Only a direct request from a senior officer would escalate the status of the test and then only if they could convince the lab that lives might be in danger if the analysis wasn't carried out quickly. She knew she had to speak to DCI McGuire anyway. She would ask him if he could pull some strings, but she hadn't been able to get hold of him as yet. He must be busy.

The images on screen were accompanied by Criminal Record Office numbers and other details that could be accessed via links, but none of the pervs she had seen so far was anything like her suspect.

It took nearly an hour to check and double check the images. It could be that the perv was from outside of the area, someone travelling in from Gwent or Dyfed Powys areas, or even further afield. Perhaps he was the owner of one of the caravans. She'd have to visit the site office and see if she could get hold of a copy of the owners' register.

It annoyed her that she couldn't remember where she had seen the man before. She had recognised him but couldn't place the face or attach a name to it. She pulled a notepad from a drawer in the desk and began to write down the facial characteristics she could remember.

> Shoulder length black hair… probably a wig.
> Angular features, probably middle aged,
> perhaps older?
> Police? Celebrity? Politician?
> Someone I know!!!!!!!!
>
>

She doodled a sad looking smiley icon under her notes, tore the page off the pad and folded it into her purse.

A visit to the site office at Trecco Bay was required.

Caroline booked out a car and drove through the lanes from Bridgend down to Porthcawl. The sun had failed to raise the temperature, but the day was crisp and clear, and the blue patches of sky were a welcome relief from the constant grey clouds that had dumped more rain in three months than Noah would have been able to deal with. But like anything good there was inevitably a negative side too. The roads were still wet, and the sun was glaring off the surface and reducing visibility to a squint.

She drove off the main road and along the entrance drive towards the Trecco Bay reception building. The place had changed a great deal over the years. A large cream-coloured building served as a reception, a lounge, a bar and a clubhouse for the complex. Play areas for children looked impressive and the whole complex looked like it had been well thought out.

Caroline pushed through the large glass doors into the bright interior of the reception. A young woman, dressed in black trousers and black polo shirt with the holiday company logo embroidered into the chest, smiled at Caroline as she strode towards the desk.

"Good afternoon, welcome to Trecco Bay Holiday Park. How can I help you?" The young woman smiled brightly.

Caroline produced her warrant card and the smile began to fade from the woman's face. "I'm PC Williams from Bridgend. I'm working on the flasher case."

The young woman looked serious and spoke in hushed tones. "Oh, thank God," she said. "I thought nobody was going to do anything with it. Can't let someone like that run around the park. Imagine if one of the kids saw him?" She made a big show of an exaggerated shiver.

Caroline nodded and lowered her voice to match the volume of the counter girl. "That's why

I'm here. I want to catch him before things get worse. Who knows what it could do to the tourist industry if this nutter isn't brought to book?"

Counter girl now looked horrified at the thought of the situation escalating.

"Ohh… mmmyyy… God," she mumbled.

"Let's hope it doesn't get that far, eh?"

The woman nodded.

Caroline moved in for the kill. "I'm worried that the flasher might be one of the owners. I wonder if I could check out the register of ownership for all the homes on the site?"

The young woman looked horrified. "I'm sorry. I don't think that's possible… it's not that I don't want to help…" she added quickly.

Caroline expected the response. "Look, I know it's probably something that's way above your pay grade, but if we're going to catch this bloke, we really need to check out every angle."

"I do understand, honestly, but…"

Caroline held up her hand. "Can you call your manager and ask for permission?"

The young woman looked like she was about to panic. "My manager is off this morning. Could you call back later?"

Shaking her head, Caroline leaned on the counter to get closer to the young woman. "You realise you could be the hero who helps to catch the flasher? I can see the headlines in all the paper…

'Holiday Park Hero catches the Dick of the Dunes.'"

The woman seemed to like the sound of that. "You think so?"

"I know so. I'll even make sure the reporters get photos of you."

She thought about it for a moment then lifted up the hatch to allow Caroline through the counter and into the back office. "I can't let you take it away, but you can use the photocopier."

Caroline smiled. "Thank you...?"

"Sarah," the young woman replied. "Sarah McDonald. That's Donald with a big 'M' and a little 'C' in front of it."

19

The follow on the Transit went without a hitch. Jane kept us up to date, every hour. The updates were for confirmation purposes only and as a backup just in case the GPS tracker device should fail. The tracker transmitter had been attached to a secret location on the Transit whilst it had been parked overnight. Not even I knew where the tracker had been hidden. The GPS receiver was installed in the car assigned to follow the van.

Jane called in after two hours on the road. "Going by the speed and manner of their driving, they should arrive in Dover about midday, just in time for the twelve-fifteen crossing. Has anyone called the port and booked the tickets for us?"

"All done," I confirmed. "They have some spare capacity on the sailing. It takes about an hour and a half to cross, so you should all arrive in Calais around two-ish?"

"Roger that," she replied, and the radio reverted to silence.

"Now we wait," I said.

***

The journey to Dover was uneventful. The follow-car and Jane's motorcycle switched places many times in the line of traffic behind the Transit. They stayed well back, which would normally be difficult for a motorcycle, especially one attempting to appear just like any other 'head-down-arse-up' rider. On two occasions she had to speed past and leave the motorway, circle on an overpass and then return behind the van and the follow-car.

They arrived at the ferry port in time for the twelve-fifteen crossing. The ferry was a colossal white vessel with six or seven deck levels above the waterline and a massive blue and white funnel stack standing proud from the rear third of the top level. It was one of those front-loader types. The whole front end of the ship had split wide open to reveal a black metal loading ramp – the black tongue of the open jaws of a monster from the deep waiting for its prey to sacrifice itself to the cavernous metal stomach.

Jane watched the Transit climb the ramp into the hold, followed by the follow-car several minutes later. Jane rode onto the deck and parked alongside several other bikes at the far end of the loading bay.

She locked her helmet in the pannier and followed other passengers up the metal enclosed staircase to the upper decks. She walked through a sliding door onto the outer deck and leaned on the handrail as she waited for completion of the loading. It took another fifteen minutes before the lines were cast and the huge engines roared into life. The whole deck began to vibrate as the ferry began to slowly pull out from the dock and head out into the English Channel.

Jane stayed on deck for the first half hour of the crossing then took a stroll through the duty-free shop and saw her two colleagues reclined on two easy chairs in a lounge off the shop. There was no acknowledgement.

She purchased a small bottle of perfume and asked for the VAT receipt and a plastic carrier bag. Armed with her 'tourist' disguise, she walked the rest of the decks and found Wilson and Bennett sitting in the lounge bar, both were sipping pints of beer.

Bloody idiots! she thought.

Jane made no eye contact, but she knew her leather gear would attract attention, so she slipped away quickly before either of the targets noticed her.

The crossing seemed to drag for Jane. She was happiest on her motorcycle and it was rare for her to take the bike out for a long run. She was itching to get back in the saddle.

The ferry docked ten minutes ahead of time and Jane called it in.

The vehicles disembarked onto the French side of the Channel and, after half an hour, the follow was on again.

It was a short run to the Cité Europe Shopping Mall and the Carrefour store.

Julie waited with her bike in the car park whilst her partners from the follow-car tailed the targets into the store. Less than an hour later, the targets returned to the van with two trollies heavily laden with booze and cigarettes. Jane did a double take when she saw her fellow officers following close behind with an equally loaded trolley of their own stock of booze and cigarettes.

She shook her head and laughed. The lads weren't going to let an opportunity like this slip through their fingers.

All vehicles loaded with duty-free, Jane followed the Transit and the police Ford Focus back to the ferry terminal for the return trip back to Blighty.

20

It had been nearly two hours since the ferry left the Port of Calais and just over thirty minutes since Jane last reported her status. Everything seemed to be going well.

I felt useless, so I poured us all a coffee and sat watching Sky News on the large flat-screen television high on the wall of the office.

Five minutes before I was expecting the next update, Jane called in. "Alpha 7 back on home soil."

I smiled. It wouldn't be long now.

The two Traffic officers gathered their kit, ready for the off. I knew one of the lads. He had been a constable on my shift when I was a sergeant in Bridgend. 'Tonto' Morris had nearly twenty years' service and was also a Special Escort Group driver, which meant he was tooled up with a Glock, used to high speed and nothing seemed to faze him. I felt guilty about his nickname. I was responsible for lumbering him with the moniker after an incident in which he received a commendation for dogged determination. He'd followed a trail of coal and dust from a stolen coal lorry up through lanes onto the mountains above Maesteg. He'd managed to find the lorry simply by driving slowly and looking for the occasion lump of coal left behind on the road when the lorry had taken a corner a bit too fast. For seven miles he had followed the trail until he found the thief already dismantling the lorry for parts in a secluded farmhouse owned by an elderly former RAF pilot. It was a clever bit of work by the officer and I was so impressed I said he must be related to Tonto. The name had stuck with him ever since, but he didn't seem to mind. I liked Tonto and knew that if the wheels came off and we ended up having to chase the bastards, Tonto would sort them out.

21

The Transit approached the sign for Leigh Delamere Services and began to slow and indicated that it was pulling in.

Jane watched the speed drop from seventy-five to fifty to forty as they moved onto the off-slip and thought they were probably stopping for a piss. It had been a long way and they hadn't had a toilet break since the ferry from Calais.

Jane slowly followed the van into the car park, staying well behind, and watched it pull up to the petrol pumps. She saw the two lemons fill the Transit with fuel. They paid for it at the convenience store and then went into the services.

She followed at a distance and saw them enter the toilets and, after several minutes, watched them pick up a pair of Starbucks before making their way to a secluded area at the rear of the car park.

Another white Transit drove slowly around the car park. It did a complete circuit, passing close by Jane before it pulled up alongside the target vehicle. The police follow-car, Alpha 6, was already on plot and had a clear view. The undercover officers were already taking dozens of images on their night-vision camera.

Jane made a note of the registration number of the new Transit; LC 06 DEL. The logo read 'Los Carbon Café and Deli,' and was emblazoned on each side of the van with a telephone number beneath.

Two eastern-European looking men got out, shook the hands of Wilson and Bennett and then began to transfer five boxes of what appeared to be wine from their van into the back of the target Transit.

The exchange took no more than three minutes and then they all shook hands again and both vehicles drove from the services.

Wilson and Bennett now had a straight run home along the M4.

This was obviously pre-planned, but it didn't make a lot of sense to Jane. She called it in and followed.

Jane and the follow-car drove across the Severn Bridge and back into Wales. The two lemons in the van still didn't have a clue as to what awaited them.

Following instructions from her radio, Jane accelerated past the follow-car and the Transit and diverted back to Barry. She was needed to do the follow on the Beemer, because the witching hour was fast approaching and the DCI wanted everything tightly packaged.

22

Jane called in when she got back to Barry in double quick time and told me she'd taken up a position a couple of streets away from the home of Dean.

She confirmed that she'd already done a drive by and the Beemer was still parked outside the target's home.

The airwaves were silent, which normally doesn't bode well. The adrenalin was pumping in the control room and I wondered how my team was handling it out on the streets. The radio commentary had to be spot on for this kind of job and it had been tight so far.

It takes a special kind of officer to carry out surveillance, you have got to be on the ball, it is stressful, but many actually seem to thrive on it. One mistake and the whole operation could go tits up.

9:29pm and the air comes alive. I get the call, "They're off, off, off. Both targets are in the target vehicle."

Jane chipped in, "I have eyeball and am following. Target vehicle travelling along College Road… Left, left, left, into St Paul's Avenue… has now joined the A4055 towards Barry Police Station… carrying on along the A4055, speed 30 mph."

The transmission was lost to static for a second

then Jane's voice crackled through again. "Target now joining the main Cardiff Road, no deviations... It's a left, left, left, into Ty Verlon Close... the target is all yours, I'm going to plot up, over."

I could hear the excitement in her voice. There was nothing more satisfying than facing dangerous situations and coming through it in one piece and with a good result. I grinned. This girl was good and what a great job she'd done for us.

The surveillance van took over the commentary, "We have the eyeball. Target vehicle has pulled up outside the unit and the two targets have alighted from the vehicle."

A short pause, I was holding my breath.

"Roller shutter doors have been raised and both targets have now entered the unit... stand by... roller shutter doors now closed and lights on inside the unit, looks like they're waiting for the van."

The air went silent for a short while and then the follow-car, Alpha 6, broke the silence, "We're on Port Road, looks like the van is making for Barry."

Five minutes later, "Alpha 6 to control? The van is approaching the Industrial Estate... it's a right, right, right, into Ty Verlon Close."

The pigeons had come home to roost.

It was now the turn of the observation van, "We have eyeball on the van, and it's pulled up outside the unit. They've honked the horn three times and the roller shutter doors have been raised... the van has now been driven inside."

This was it.

I heard a voice shout into the microphone, "Strike, strike, strike!"

***

Police officers of all shapes, sizes and descriptions; short ones, tall ones, fat ones, thin ones, smart ones and scruffy bastards, all suddenly swamped the industrial unit, as if by magic.

Firearms officers spend years training for incidents such as these. A fit looking heavily armed officer in black coveralls and body armour began to shout, "Armed Police! Get out of the vehicle, put your hands on your heads and lie on the ground. Do it now!"

Wilson and Bennett stepped slowly out of the Transit and then, together with Dean and Smith, scattered in all directions, like the Red Arrows on one of their break manoeuvres. The five armed-response officers held their fire. There was no sign of weapons and no justification to use them.

Most normal people, faced with five hairy-arsed and heavily armed coppers, would do as they were told, but not this lot of muppets, they were out of the lock-up and doing fair impressions of Usain Bolt. The thought of serious bird could cause some pretty crazy reactions in people and it was either that or they were doped up to their eyeballs.

Wilson and Bennett were brought to ground by squad boys, Tim and Karl, and poor old Smith found himself wrestling with the old German shepherd that quickly got the upper paw and had him by the balls, good and proper.

Colin pulled into the car park in the back seat of Tonto's Traffic car, a fully marked, three-litre BMW five-series. Tonto screeched to a halt near the chaos and Colin dropped the rear window to get a better look at the action.

"They can count themselves lucky it's Wales, Sarge. If this was the States, they'd have copped a double-tap from a nine-mill by now," Tonto observed.

Colin agreed. "Aye, we tend to prefer them alive, doesn't matter how fucked up it gets."

Colin began to clamber out of the back seat when he saw Dean doubling back and make for the Beemer.

"The car!" Colin shouted to the mass of writhing bodies struggling to control the prisoners, but he could see there was nobody with a hand free let alone a pair of legs to put up a chase. "Fuck!"

Dean started the car and screamed a donut on the car park before racing past the Traffic car and nearly wiping out a couple of the squad.

As he roared out of the estate, the second Traffic car appeared as Tonto put his car into reverse, slammed his foot hard down on the throttle and then spun the steering around. The front end of the car swung around neatly as Tonto found first gear and took off after the fleeing BMW.

"Fuck me, what was that?" Colin shouted from

the foot well as he struggled to pull himself back into the seat to fasten his belt.

"That's what we call a J-turn, Sarge."

Colin swallowed back the rising vomit and called for the dog handler to follow at a safe speed so that the old German shepherd could have its fun again if Dean managed to get away from Traffic. But Tonto had other ideas.

The target BMW squealed past a performance bike sales unit and along Sully View.

Tonto had a lot of ground to make up on the car, but he smoothly accelerated through the gears and kept the target in sight as his radio operator began calling in the action.

"Got 'em now, Sarge," Tonto shouted to Colin. "It's a dead end, whichever direction he takes."

The brake lights flashed on ahead and Tonto slammed on the brakes. The target did a handbrake in front of them and Tonto steered the BMW towards the approaching car. At the last moment, the target car swerved left, up onto the pavement and squeezed past. Tonto pulled the handbrake and slid his car around.

"Shit!" Tonto shouted. "Les will stop him."

Les Davies, the driver of the other Traffic car was some distance behind and slid the car sideways to block the road. The target didn't slow. Dean veered to the right and struck the back end of Les' car, smashing it out of the way.

Tonto slowed momentarily alongside Les. The

thumbs up signal was all he needed to know his mate was safe and he slammed his foot back on the throttle and raced after Dean. Dean turned left from Sully View onto Cardiff Road and drove straight into the side of a heavy panel van. The back end of the van disintegrated and so did the front end of the BMW.

Tonto slammed on the brakes and Colin leapt from the back and ran to the driver's door. Dean was lying against the steering wheel. The airbag had exploded in his face and Dean was out for the count. Colin could see the front end of the car had been pushed back into Dean's legs, but he was still breathing.

***

With Smith, Wilson and Bennett cuffed and secure, the moment of truth had come. They had all been arrested for conspiracy to supply class A drugs.

Steve donned a pair of latex gloves and opened the back doors of the van. It was full of cartons of cigarettes and the six-pack boxes of wine – dozens of them.

He noticed that the first five boxes looked out of place with the rest, he didn't bother opening any of them, he just cleared the lock-up and called for the drugs dog.

Within a few minutes the handler had the brown and white spaniel on a short leash and the dog began sniffing around the outside of the van before jumping onto the load bay. The dog sniffed around the boxes and then went crazy. The handler struggled to pull him from the van. "That didn't take long," he said. "I think you've got a shed-full in there, Sarge."

Steve then carefully opened one of the boxes, took out the six bottles of wine and there at the bottom were four neatly wrapped packs of white powder.

Result.

The other four boxes were exactly the same. Steve then had them removed and photographed. Then just to be on the safe side, he had the drug dog put back inside. The only thing he did this time was piss up against the cartons of cigarettes.

The team were called together, and Steve reminded them of the instructions regarding the prisoner transportation to Bridgend and the recovery of the van and drugs.

***

I heard the news of the result and jumped into the air, accidentally punched my fist through a suspended ceiling tile. I was over the moon with the result but would not be one hundred per cent satisfied until I had the full details on Dean's condition and I had the bastard locked up. That could well be some time if his injuries were serious.

23

"I'm sorry I didn't get back to you earlier," I told Caroline. She sat in a spare chair in the office I borrowed in headquarters, legs crossed and arms folded. She looked uneasy.

I borrowed an office away from the squad and division in the hope that the meeting would remain between the two of us.

"You OK?"

"Er, yes, sir... I mean, boss."

I smiled. She remembered.

"I need you to do a little job for me. I know you're keen to do an aide on the department, but that fell flat when I moved over on promotion."

"Yes, boss," she agreed.

"Well, I feel bad about that. I'll see what I can do. I'll call the DI on division and ask him to give you a shot."

She smiled. "Thank you, boss."

"In return, I'd like you to carry out a little undercover work."

She looked intrigued.

"Before you agree to it you need to know that everything I say to you today is off the record and highly classified. Do you understand?"

She looked unsure but nodded. "Yes, boss."

"Do you know a guy on my squad called the Hulk?"

"The bodybuilder?"

"That's the one."

"Yes. I know of him. Never met him though. Paths never crossed."

"Good," I said, relieved that I hadn't fallen at the first hurdle. It was vital that the Hulk didn't know Caroline either. "Do you think he'd know you?"

"Wouldn't think so, boss."

"This is important. Are you sure?"

"As sure as I can be."

I stood from my chair and walked to the door. I put my ear to the door then opened it to check outside. It was clear. I returned to my seat.

"This sounds serious?" Caroline said.

I shrugged. "It is and it isn't. Or, rather, it could be. It's a pile of shit, to be honest."

She looked curious.

"One of my lads has been put in the frame for steroid abuse and a little dealing of the juice..."

"The Hulk?"

"You got it. He's obviously on some shit. He's unpredictable, prone to moods and I can't have someone like that on the squad."

"And where do I come in, boss?"

"Do you work out? You look fit..." I felt myself blush when I realised what I'd said. "...I mean, you look like you keep yourself fit?"

Caroline laughed. "I understood what you meant, boss. Don't worry. And, yes. I do go to the gym. Got to do it these days."

"Good," I said. I felt the blood drain away from my face. "I'd like you to do your training in the..." I had to check my notes, "...Best Bodies Gym down on Walcott Road. Do you know it?"

She nodded. "Been in there a few times. Need a membership to enter and I don't have one."

"Don't worry about that. Join up and bring me the bill. I'll sort it."

"And what do you want me to do there? I assume you want me to keep an eye out for your boy?"

"That's it. I just want you to train there, keep a discreet eye on the Hulk and report back whatever you see the bastard doing. Is that alright with you?"

She looked unsure.

"Worried about snitching on a colleague?"

"Yes, boss."

"No need to worry. Nobody will know, it's just you and me. You won't be used for evidence. I just want to confirm my suspicions before I do anything else and don't come near me. There's a chance the Hulk will see you so make sure you ring me on this number." I gave her the number I had scribbled on a PostIt Note.

"OK, boss. I'll do it."

I grinned. "Great."

She stood. "Before I go... is there any chance you could add a bit of weight to pushing a DNA sample through the lab?"

"DNA, what's it all about?"

"It's that fucking flasher, boss. The Cock of the Walk..."

"The Dick of the Dunes," I sniggered as I reminded her of the unofficial tag we'd given the flasher.

"That's the one," she said. "I almost had him, but he ran off and dropped a paper tissue. He had a tissue in his hand as he was... well, you know?"

"I know," I agreed.

"Well, I recovered the tissue and it was... damp," she grimaced at the thought.

She didn't have to say anymore. "I'll call the lab and ask them to expedite it."

She smiled. "Thanks, boss."

"No," I said. "Thank you. I never forget favours."

24

It was early Tuesday morning and I was making my way to the Moor to have a chat with Steve Diamond about Coulter. DI Coulter was convicted around the same time as Cliff Ambrose. He'd been involved in some serious 'fit-up' jobs and also a rape on a former prostitute. I left my team to sort out the paperwork for the drugs bust and was happy to travel down to Dartmoor alone.

Steve and I had spoken some time ago when I was investigating the corrupt practices of my old friends and former colleagues. Steve Diamond had given me enough rope to hang former DCI Cliff Ambrose but had intimated that there was more to be told about Coulter and that he'd give me more after they were potted. I was keen to discover any other corrupt practices the traitorous bastard had been up to.

I did also promise Steve that if we potted Coulter I'd try and get him placed nearer home because his missus and kids were finding the trek down to the West Country nigh on impossible.

My biggest problem was that, because of what had been going on, I hadn't had the time to clear it all up.

I had no idea how to play this. The bloke wasn't dull and seemed to be able to read people like a book. After letting him down regarding the move I wasn't expecting a warm welcome.

I arrived at 10 a.m. and the Governor came to meet me and he was just as amenable as the last time I was there. Fair play to him, he invited me back to his office for a cup of coffee. This was not normal practice but, hey, you can't beat a bit of networking and you never know, I may want a favour in the future.

It seemed that the Governor was interested in the Ambrose and Coulter cases too. I think he was on the same page as me. He obviously hated any form of corruption.

"I'll help anyway I can," he said. "If we can root out the corrupt bastards in our services it would make life much easier for all the good officers... of which there are many, I'm glad to say."

I couldn't agree more.

He then picked up the phone and ordered that Diamond be taken to the interview room.

The Governor shook my hand, "I'll be gone when you're done, Terry. I'm afraid I've got yet another talking shop conference I can't get out of."

One of the officers led me to the interview room. Steve was already there and he was smiling like the Cheshire Cat. I shook his hand and gave him a packet of Bensons.

Before I opened my mouth, he said, "Thank you, Terry, you're a man of your word. They're shipping me to Swansea nick tomorrow."

I had nothing to do with it, but I recognised an

opportunity I could exploit. "No problem, Steve," I said. "As long as you're happy with that?"

"I'll be able to see my family more often then. I may get out in another fifteen, if I'm lucky."

I nodded. I didn't want to say anything to mess things up. Things looked promising.

"Any time with the family is important to me. It'll keep me going, and you've done me a favour I won't forget. Now, let's get down to business."

I felt a bit of a twat but, then again, this bloke was a killer.

"Any idea where Coulter was getting his cash from?" I asked. "He had about four-hundred grand in various accounts that were off shore."

He smiled. "Well, it wasn't from any jobs I did with him. Yeah, he was pulling a few grand here and there, but not that kind of bread."

I was disappointed. Was this going to be a wasted trip after all? "Have you any idea at all?"

"No idea about amounts like that, I can only think he was involved with bigger fish than me. You know his track record, he was always going abroad, Spain, Amsterdam, France perhaps he was at it over there? I don't know and I don't really care."

I felt embarrassed. I didn't want to let on to Steve that we hadn't put that one together. "Yeah, sounds feasible, Steve. Fair play," I said.

"Did he ever mention anything that he was involved with abroad, any jobs or anything?"

"No, but knowing him he would probably tip

the villains off for a backhander."

"I need a little more than that," I said. Steve could see I was disappointed.

He thought for a moment. "He was always banging on about antiques and all that bollocks. I wasn't interested in all that crap so never really paid him much attention. The only artist I know is Rolf Harris and the only painting he's doing of late is the shithouse in the pokey since he got locked up."

Antiques? The Dutch man came to mind. Bingo! Connection.

"Look, Terry, I think we've all got what we wanted, shall we knock it on the head? I gave you the conviction, you got me home, fair trade, I think?"

Steve then put his hand out to shake. I thought why not, let's close the book on Coulter and Ambrose. I had enough on my plate as it was.

As I stood to leave, Steve opened his pack of cigarettes and handed one to me to light for him. "Mind you, Terry, if I do hear anything down your neck of the woods, anything tidy that is, I'll deffo give you a bell."

I nodded. "I'll keep you to that. Keep safe, Steve," I said.

"You too, Terry, you too. It's been a pleasure. More coppers like you they need, butt."

I left the prison and took a short drive around the local village, caught a cup of coffee to drink in the car and then began the long drive home.

The trip to see Steve had not given me anymore that I could use against Coulter or Cliff Ambrose, but I spent the rest of the time thinking about the team doing the interviews, about the threat Molly had received. I thought about the Hulk, the Dutchman, and all sorts of shit that I would rather not think about.

It was just another ordinary day in the head of Terry McGuire.

25

Caroline checked her communication from the lab for the fourth time. They had a positive DNA sample from the flasher's paper tissue but no match with anyone known on the database. That was disappointing but at least it meant the Sword of Damocles was now hanging over the bastard and it would only be a matter of time before it fell. She hoped that when it did fall it would chop off his 'old boy.'

She stuffed the report into the glove box of her car and set the alarm. She jogged the last mile to the gym, hoping the sweat she'd generate on the way would convince the usual gym-monkeys that she was one of them. She'd already created a membership online and printed the receipt to claim the cost back, as suggested by McGuire.

The gym was quieter than she'd expected. The large area containing the various machines was less than a quarter full; that equated to about eight juicers pumping away and posing in the multitude of mirrors affixed to all the walls. It was a poser's paradise. There was more love present in that place than the Sistine Chapel, but all the love was narcissistic.

She tried to ignore the prima donnas and found an empty running machine. She set the speed and time for a fast jog for twenty minutes and loaded her plastic water container into a cup holder built into the chassis. Everything had to have a cup holder these days. Car salesmen even mentioned them in their pitch to prospective buyers.

The machine began to build up speed. She checked the wall mirror to get a better look at the iron-pumpers behind her. No sign of the Hulk. She knew that surveillance often meant hours, if not days or weeks of fruitless effort. She had to become a regular to blend into the background. That wasn't going to happen for a while. She could feel the eyes of the men who favoured the female flesh boring into her. She began to wish she hadn't worn the tight leggings.

There was just under five minutes left on her pre-set run when the Hulk entered. She had seen him before but hoped he hadn't noticed her. Even if he did, there was no reason to suspect that she was there to watch him.

The Hulk looked her way, let his eyes linger a little too long, and then did a quick stretch before loading huge discs of iron onto a bench press. Her view of him in the mirror was excellent. He was framed perfectly. Rather than change machine, she reset the timer for another twenty minutes. Her thighs were beginning to burn but her breathing was still steady.

The Hulk pumped out eight slow reps and let the bar crash back down onto the bench stand. He sat upright and loosened his arms with rolls and stretches and then stood to admire himself in a nearby mirror.

Satisfied at what could only have been microscopic increases in his bulk, he lay back down and pushed out ten more. This time, she could hear him grunting with the exertion.

The Hulk moved between apparatus, carrying out what Caroline assumed was a targeted routine.

She couldn't run anymore so found a cycling machine with an equally good view of the gym in the mirror.

At the end of a serious set of leg presses, the Hulk checked his watch, wiped himself down and stepped outside.

Caroline stopped her cycle and walked out to the reception where she grabbed herself a waxed paper cone and filled it with water from a fountain. She stood in the entrance door and sipped from the cup. The Hulk was outside talking to a young man sitting behind the wheel of a pimped-up Astra. The Hulk took a small package from a pocket in his shorts and handed it through the open window. She saw the driver hand the Hulk what looked like bank notes.

26

I got to the office, late afternoon. Mike was there, with a broad smile, the cat that got the cream.

"How's it all panning out, Mike? Are we making progress?"

It was Mike's turn to make the coffee. I just hoped he'd improved his skills. He stood over the percolator and the smells of freshly brewing coffee brought a deep sigh and smile from me.

"Yes," he said. "The interviews are going well, they're all putting their hands up. I personally think that Dean is the main player. Smith is a bit of a gopher for him and as for the other two? I heard the word 'lemons' was mentioned? I would plump for 'dick heads.' We had to have the police doctor out a couple of times for them, especially for the dog bite to one of the clown's nuts; they've been crawling up the walls. They've settled a bit now. But as we suspected, it's cocaine, about ten kilos, value of around four-hundred grand. God knows the street value after it's cut. The lab tells me it's cracking stuff, not far off one hundred per cent pure and by far the best shit the squad have dealt with. I reckon it's direct from South America."

I was impressed but not as excited as I thought I'd be. Perhaps it was the whole business of the threat to Molly? "I take it the boys are doing the business on the two foreigners and the other Transit van?"

Mike nodded.

"That could be very interesting. Anyway, I'll leave it to you, Mike. I know I can rely on you."

Mike handed me a large mug of freshly brewed beans. He seems to have picked up on my mood. "Are you OK, Terry? You haven't been yourself the last couple of days. You should be over the moon. You got the squad back on track and they trust you. The consensus amongst the team is that they should have had you as boss years ago."

I sipped the steaming coffee and felt an instant buzz. "I'm OK, butt. I'm a bit concerned about Molly and that phone call, that's all. Look I'm going to finish this and then shoot off home. I've had a long day, all that driving. Give my best to the squad, tell them I'll be in early tomorrow."

I got home about 6 o'clock. Molly was preparing a bit of supper, not a cooked dinner, just chips and a tin of salmon.

I walked into the kitchen and gave her a squeeze as she was opening the tin, she turned, and I could see she'd been crying.

"I had another one of those calls this morning, Terry. He was really evil this time, threatened the same, and said he was going to blow you away and do things to me, then just hung up."

I was seething. I tried to remain calm, not to make Molly feel any worse than she already did.

"Anything in his voice that stood out, Molly?"

She tucked her head into my shoulder. "He sounded either Scottish or Irish, more Scottish I would think."

I sighed. Considering the number of years I'd served, we'd been pretty lucky. I'd only ever been threatened once before and the guy had come off second best. But nobody had ever brought their shit to my door and upset my wife. "Molly, Molly, Molly, I'm so sorry, I'll find the bastard and I'll rip his throat out and stuff his phone down the soggy end."

Molly laughed but also knew I was serious. "Be careful, Terry. Don't do anything silly. It's only a crank call."

I felt like my head was about to explode, my blood pressure must have been reaching danger levels. I had thoughts that I never even knew I could imagine. I pictured myself killing someone. I didn't give a shit about myself, but my Molly? I had to keep her safe.

We managed to cool down enough to be functional, even if it was only at a level that was more mechanical than anything else. At least we had our supper. We were both drained and climbed the stairs for an early night.

I tried to read the new book Molly had bought me, some old bollocks about an ex Swansea cop caught up in the search for the Eden Relics, when Molly rolled over and cwtshed up to me. "You haven't forgotten about tomorrow, Terry?"

I shut my eyes, desperately trying to figure out what I'd forgotten; anniversary, birthday? I had to own up. "Sorry, love?"

"My car is booked in for the MOT?"

I felt relieved. "Oh aye, leave it to me. You can have mine to do your shopping and I'll drop yours up to the garage first thing in the morning. One of their lads will run me to the nick. They're pretty good like that. You can have a nice lie in." I kissed her gently on the top of her head and lay awake thinking about what I'd like to do to the scum threatening us. I heard Molly's breathing becoming deeper. At least she'd found peace. It was going to be a long night for me.

First thing in the morning, I took Molly's eight-year-old Ford Ka to the local garage. The car wasn't worth much, but it was her pride and joy and she always took care of it. The boys in the garage knew the car, it had been serviced regularly with them since new. I was confident it would fly through the roadworthy test. The chief mechanic, Andy, assured me they'd call for Molly later in the day when the car was ready for collection. One of the apprentice mechanics drove me to our home in Kingshill, a nice, quiet part of Porthcawl. We'd lived there for nearly twenty-five years and I couldn't see us ever wanting to move. The fact that someone had invaded our privacy and had entered our home, albeit via the telephone line, was something that deeply concerned me.

One of the local uniform boys was waiting for me when the garage truck dropped me at the end of the street. The panda car was parked on my drive, and he dropped me off at the office around 9 am.

The office was buzzing with activity. All the team members were writing their statements and tying up all the loose ends. Heads were down over desks and the sound of fingers clicking on keyboards was only outdone by the tunes coming from Radio 2. My two DS's were down the Bridewell Detention Centre with the interview officers.

This is what I loved about policing; it was like watching a nest of ants at work, all labouring towards a common objective.

I was in my office off the main team room when Mike came in and shut the door.

He didn't have to be asked for coffee, he'd brought two cups with him and placed them on the desk. I was becoming addicted to this bean machine and Mike was getting better at making it.

"You OK, boss?"

I reclined in my chair and wondered what I should say. I'm not one to open up to anyone. I tell Molly more things than anyone else, but I don't even tell her everything. I've always believed it was my place to shoulder the burden and to try and protect my family and friends from things that might hurt them. It often resulted in me feeling pretty low from time to time, but, as a husband, a father and a team leader, I always put a brave face on things. Molly could always tell when I was worried, but she also knew I had to deal with things in my own way. Selfish? Probably.

"Molly had another call yesterday," I finally admitted. "Same bloke by the sounds of it. A Jock, I think? Threatened the burn again and also talked about blowing me away and doing things to Molly." I watched Mike's eyes widen in surprise. "Mike, I tell you, butt, I'll fucking kill the bastard if he comes near Molly or me."

Mike sat forward, leaning closer to me. I'd seen and used the technique many times; show interest and build a connection to the subject but I knew this was just a normal and genuine reaction from Mike. "Cool down now, Terry. We've got a lot to sort out. Why don't you go home? Spend the day with Molly. Perhaps you'll feel a bit better? I can handle things here."

I smiled, grateful for his concern. "No, she'll be off shopping up in Pyle later and she's got my Audi,"

Mike laughed. "You let her use your Audi? Fuck, mate. You are rattled."

I didn't laugh. "Aye. I hope to fuck she doesn't prang it."

As the morning progressed, I barely stepped outside my office. I wasn't functioning well; couldn't concentrate. This thing with Molly was eating me up. Mike kept me updated on the case progress from time to time and eventually told me that charges were imminent and that a special court had been arranged for the next day for the remands.

I was genuinely pleased for the team. "Cracking, Mike. That's great, butt. I'm pleased for the squad and everyone involved. Tell them once this is all put to bed, I'll be buying the beer for everyone."

The phone on my desk rang and Mike picked up. I could tell by his expression and silence that something had gone tits up. He handed the phone to me. "It's for you, Terry. It's Tony Traffic... it's about Molly..."

I snatched the phone from Mike's hand. "Hello? Terry McGuire here."

"Sorry to call you like this, sir. It's Tony Evans from Traffic. I'm afraid to tell you that Mrs McGuire's been involved in an accident..."

My blood ran cold. "A what? Is she OK, how did it happen, Tony?"

"I think she'll be fine, don't worry, she's in good hands. It seems she crashed the car in Porthcawl. She's in a bit of a bad way but nothing life threatening. The doc said she's fractured her sternum, broken one of her arms..."

I covered the mouthpiece. I could see Mike wanted an update. "Fuck me, Mike, she's been in a crash. Broken sternum and arm," I said.

I got the rest of the information from Tony and thanked him before I hung up.

"I'm taking a pool car to the hospital and I'll let

you know the score as soon as I do," I told Mike.

I arrived at the Princes of Wales Casualty Department and saw two Traffic cars outside and a herd of ambulances; nothing unusual there.

The unit was packed out to the gunnels, but I spotted Tony Evans. He walked over to me and shook my hand. "She's had one hell of a wallop, boss. The doctor's with her now. She's conscious. Like I said on the phone, she's got a fractured sternum, broken arm but luckily no head injuries. The seat belt saved her there."

"Where did it happen, Tony?"

"On the nasty right-hander past the Grove Golf Club, on the way into Porthcawl. Looks like Mrs McGuire lost it completely, went straight on, clipped an on-comer and flew through the hedge."

I cringed at the thought of my wife going through all that. "Oh fuck, Tony. Where's the car now?"

"'Poachers Recovery' towed it in."

I began to wonder about the timing of this. Could it just be a coincidence that we get death threats and a day later my wife ends up in Casualty? I didn't bloody think so, not for a sodding minute.

"Right, do me a favour? Give 'Poachers' a ring and tell them not to touch it. Could you have one of your examiners to go through it with a fine toothcomb? I'll arrange for SOCO to confer with your boy."

"Listen, boss, I've finished here, I'll see to this

myself," Tony was puzzled. "What are you thinking?"

"I don't know, Tony, but trust me on this one. I'll get Glyn Walcott up there asap to confer with you."

"I'm on it, boss. Leave it to me."

I used my job mobile to give Glyn the SOCO a ring. I filled him in about my suspicions and he dropped everything to make the examination a priority.

I knew there was more to this than just a psycho Jock who had picked me out of the phonebook for special psycho attention. The only person I could think of who might have been behind this was my former colleague, Cliff. If he was involved, I swore he'd end up dead.

***

I managed to eventually speak to the duty doctor. He couldn't tell me any more than what Tony Traffic had told me.

"Can I see her, Doc?"

"Of course you can, she's been banged about a bit, but all her vitals are strong and steady, no head trauma. I'm confident she'll make a full recovery, but it'll take a while."

I thanked the doctor and shook his hand. The conflicting emotions of anger and relief were almost overwhelming.

I entered the recovery room and found my Molly wired up to the monitors, arm in plaster with her eyes closed. I could feel the tears well in my eyes and couldn't help thinking she'd been so lucky, even though she didn't exactly look very lucky at that time.

I kissed her head, sat by her side and held her hand and then the floodgates opened, and I began to cry.

I could tell you the exact dates I have cried. The last time was three years ago on September the 23rd when my Mam passed away. This was different. This was the love of my life, my soul mate, the woman who had stood by me through thick and thin and I had failed in what I had always considered to be my primary purpose – to protect her.

Molly opened her eyes and squeezed my hand. She whispered, "I love you, tell the kids I'm OK, there's no need for them to come home."

I managed to say, "I love you too," before my Molly drifted off to sleep again. A smiling and sympathetic young nurse entered with two porters. "I have to take her to the IC unit now, Mr McGuire. She'll be more comfortable there and they'll look after her, don't worry."

I wiped my eyes, thanked the young nurse and left Molly in her capable hands.

I dreaded my next task. I had to tell the kids. What could you say when they live half way around the world with their families?

I called Christian first. I told him what had

happened. He was shocked and wanted to come home, but I told him what Molly would wish them to know and that meant I watered it down quite a bit. I made no mention of my suspicions. What good would it do? Chris was clearly feeling anxious. I tried to calm him down by asking him about his work and he told me he was in the middle of a deal that was vital to his construction company. That settled it as far as I was concerned, I forbade him from coming home. He eventually saw my point of view and asked me to ring him every day with updates.

I managed to get through to Carmel on the fourth attempt. She was distraught and I felt so helpless. I wanted to cwtsh her and to tell her everything would be all right. She eventually calmed down and I agreed that I'd ring her every day, too. It made it easier for me to know that they were good kids and respected our wishes for them to stay put and that there was no immediate danger to them either. I kept my fingers crossed the whole time. If things took a turn for the worse, I'd have an awful lot to explain.

Brought up in an immigrant Irish family, Catholicism had always been a part of my early life. Like others of my age, as a child I attended church each Sunday and went to all the festivals. I remembered that there were a lot of festivals. By the time I reached my teens I'd had enough of festivals. My local priest was a really good guy. He tried to make services fun for all the kids, and I liked him. But as I grew up, I found it impossible to rationalise the hypocrisy of organised religion, not just Catholic but *all* religions, and I wanted nothing to do with any of them. That had been my stance ever since. But even I couldn't fail to recognise the hypocrisy of *my* actions when I sat in the hallway outside the ICU and began to pray for my Molly.

***

I was shredded by the time I called Mike and updated him.

With all my essential chores completed, I drove down to 'Poachers' in Cornelly. I pulled up and parked on the road outside the garage and before I got out of the car, both Glyn and Tony rushed over to me. My poor beloved Audi was up on the hydraulic ramp.

I felt a deep dread and could tell by Tony's face that things were dodgy. "You've got to see this, boss," he said.

I followed Tony and Glyn and stepped under what was left of my car.

Tony pointed to the brake lines. "Your brake pipes have been cut in four places, boss. Glyn and I are both agreed on that."

"No doubt, boss," Glyn confirmed.

"Someone's out to get you, boss, and that's for sure," Tony said.

I stepped out from under the car. I wanted to scream in rage, but a strange calm then seemed to descend upon me, and things suddenly began to fall into place. I would kill the bastard. Of that there was no doubt. Now all I needed to do was find out who was behind it and put the twat out of his misery once and for all.

I was surprisingly cool enough to function. The idea of topping the bastard had suddenly lifted a burden from my shoulders. I would be snatching back the masculinity the bastard had stolen from me when I was unable to protect Molly. I think Tony was surprised by my calm demeanour. I asked him to arrange for the vehicle to be taken to the underground garage at HQ for storage.

"No worries, boss." He said. "The boys in the garage will see to that for me, they're good as gold."

Mike was waiting for me when I returned to the office. He'd got some of the uniform lads to pick up Molly's Ka from the MOT station and I was grateful. Silly little things like that can make a big difference when someone is stressed. I filled him in, but both of us could only guess at who could be behind it.

"Could it be Cliff?" he suggested.

"It had crossed my mind. To be honest, I don't think he has the balls to go after me."

"Well, perhaps it's best to let the local lads deal with it? Don't do anything silly."

I said nothing. Mike looked at me as if he was trying to read my mind.

"Seriously, Terry. Don't do anything daft."

I took the bottle of malt from my drawer and poured a larger than normal shot into my grubby glass. It burned as it passed down my throat, but it was good. I filled the glass again and offered Mike a fill.

"No thanks, boss. Take it easy on that stuff, especially if you're driving. Perhaps I should call a uniform to run you down there?"

"Don't fucking patronise me," I snapped through gritted teeth.

Mike held up his hand. "Sorry, boss. Didn't mean to…"

I shook my head and stopped him. I had no idea what had come over me. I realised Mike was trying to help. "Sorry, Mike. Sorry. I don't know what's wrong with me. I'm so wound up over this Molly thing…"

Mike nodded. "I know, Terry, you should take time off. When Molly gets out, take her away somewhere."

I smiled but knew that wouldn't happen.

I ran through the case file and checked with Jeff on progress of the statements whilst Mike went off to meet with the CPS. I had no intention of staying long. I just couldn't concentrate. Less than two hours later, I was donning my coat and heading for the door as Mike returned.

"I'm off to see Molly now, Mike, I'm sorry about all this, but I know you have it all under control."

"No problem, Terry. We're charging tonight, then court in the morning. All the paperwork is now sorted, at least that's what Jeff just told me, and I've had a conference with the CPS. The four fuckers aren't going anywhere for a while."

I nodded. "I'll probably stay with Molly 'till the early hours, Mike." I shook his hand and thanked him for all his support.

***

I sat in the pool car in the station car park and trawled through the list of contacts on my mobile. Caroline, the policewoman, was next on my call list. She answered on the second ring.

"Any update?"

"I think so, boss."

"You think so?"

"I saw him outside the gym, passing a packet over to a guy in one of those boy-racer Astras. The driver passed what I think was money back to him."

"Shit! I was afraid of that. Did you get the registration number?"

"Yes, boss."

Caroline gave me the number of the car and I tapped it into the police national computer facility recently installed in the dash of the CID vehicle. "Hang on," I said. I waited a few moments for the owner details to appear. "The owner is a chap called Sam Hitchings... looks like he's got a bit of form for drugs and minor theft."

I heard Caroline curse on the other end of the line.

I didn't want her involved any further. This was a job for Professional Standards. "Leave it with me, Caroline. I'll sort it out. Thanks for your help."

"No problem, sir. Sorry the news isn't good."

"So am I," I agreed.

Then I remembered the flasher. "Did you get the result of the DNA test?"

"Yes, boss. A good DNA profile but no match to anyone on our system."

"So, we have a virgin?"

She laughed. "I guess you could say that."

We finished the call with a promise from me that an aide to CID would be forthcoming and I had a mate on division who would look after her. I needed to tie all the loose ends together first.

I called DS Dai Williams, my former right-hand-man. We had worked together on the Coulter and Ambrose cases and there was nobody I trusted more.

Dai had already heard about Molly. He sounded shocked and apologised for not calling me first. I told him I understood and that the prognosis was good.

"How's *your* married life?" I asked.

"Pretty good, Terry, surprisingly."

We both chuckled. This was Dai's third marriage and knowing him I didn't hold out much hope of him celebrating an anniversary of any great significance.

"You're not calling me for news of my sex life, are you?"

"You could illuminate me, if you wish," I joked.

"Fuck off, you old perv,'" he laughed.

"I'm actually calling you to see if you could do

me a favour, no, two favours, actually."

"Oh?"

I ran through what I knew about the Hulk and asked him to sort out some kind of sting on the bastard. I also asked him to sort out an aide for Caroline. I could hear the change in his tone when I mentioned an attractive potential aide on his team. "Don't even think about it," I warned. "She's not your type."

"Don't know what you mean, boss? I'm a happily married man," he said.

I found the notes I had on the Hulk and sent them via a private message to Dai and then set off for the hospital again.

It took me twenty minutes to get to a parking spot in the busy car park and another ten minutes to find my way back to the ward I left her in earlier. I spoke to the staff on the ward desk and they kindly brought me an easy chair.

I sat by the side of the bed and I held Molly's hand. She stirred but didn't wake. I was suddenly exhausted; the stress finally wiped the legs away from under me. I lay my head on the bed beside my wife. I knew that Molly was safe and I quietly promised her once more that I would find and kill the bastard responsible. Then I drifted off to a troubled sleep.

27

DI Mike Johnston had nothing but respect for Terry. He'd known him for many years and he knew that Terry McGuire was a 'copper's copper.' He was dedicated, honest and wouldn't hesitate to help anyone. However, over the last day or so he'd been seeing a different side to Terry.

Molly's accident had pushed him near the edge, his behaviour was bordering on the obsessive, he seemed paranoid about Cliff Ambrose, and it was clear to Mike that Terry believed Cliff was the one pulling the strings, even though he was banged up in the nick.

Mike had never heard Terry threatening to kill anyone before, but that had all changed. It seemed to be the only thing on his mind.

Terry's rapidly declining state of mental health was a worry. He looked about to go off the deep end. He had to help his friend and the only thing he could think of was to arrange a private meeting with the ACC.

As soon as Mike explained his concerns, the ACC told him meet him at headquarters as soon as possible. Within twenty minutes, Mike entered the ACC's office and stood to attention.

The ACC directed Mike to a chair. "What's the problem with him, Mike? It must be important to take you away from the current enquiry."

"Yes, sir, it is. You know the chief's wife has been having crank telephone calls at home from some Scottish bastard, threatening to torch the house and top Terry?"

The ACC looked shocked. "How many calls?"

"Only two, sir. But there's also now the accident that Molly was involved in. Molly was driving Terry's car and the brake pipes had been cut. Molly was lucky to survive."

"I'm aware of the accident. Terry informed me about it, but nothing about the phone calls."

Mike nodded. "Well, I think Terry is losing it, sir. He's getting paranoid about Cliff Ambrose; he thinks that he's behind all this grief."

The ACC snorted. "Unlikely, don't you think?"

Mike shrugged. "The mood he's in, I think if he finds out who's responsible, he might top 'em, sir."

"Surely not? He can't be that bad, Mike?"

"I think he is, sir. I'm keeping him on the level at the moment, but you know what he's like."

"Oh yes, I know what Terry is like, Mike. He's a good, solid, honest copper. I just can't see him doing anything stupid."

"I hope you're right, sir."

The ACC sat back in his high-back leather chair and pondered for a moment. He clearly wasn't sure Terry wouldn't do something stupid. Everybody had a tipping point. He'd seen good officers lose it before for less provocation than Terry was facing.

"What do you suggest?" he asked.

"I don't like going behind Terry's back, sir. It seems disloyal..."

"Spit it out, Mike. This is not disloyalty, you're trying to look after a friend and colleague, who you believe is on the edge. That's what I call friendship. If you're unsure you need to ask yourself something..."

"What's that?"

"Are you unsure because you don't want to get your friend into trouble or are you unsure because you don't know how your colleagues will react to you bringing your concerns to me?"

That hit Mike hard. Truth was he knew it was for both reasons.

The ACC let him think a moment and could see the turmoil in his expression. "What do you want me to do, Mike?" he said softly.

Mike sighed. This was going to be awkward. "Can we monitor his house landline and his office phone? I'm sure he'll have more calls. We need to know what Terry knows and we need to have the drop on whoever is doing this."

"To what end, Mike?"

"Well, I don't want him having any calls from this scumbag that will set him off like a loose cannon, because I honestly think that this is what it's all leading up to. Whoever it is, they are really winding him up. I'm very worried about Terry. He's becoming irrational. Work-wise he's still pretty spot on, a bit distracted but he doesn't miss a thing. As for the rest? He's off his box."

The ACC looked worried. The last thing any police force wanted was to be embroiled in an officer meltdown. "I like and respect Terry, Mike. I don't want to lose him like this... leave it with me. I'll sort all the necessary with the phones. If there are any calls that might trigger him, you'll be informed, any hour of the day. Is that OK with you?"

Mike sighed and forced a smile. "Thank you, sir."

As he rose to leave, the ACC stood and shook his hand. "Terry and the squad are lucky to have someone like you to look after their backs..."

"Thank you, sir, but I don't feel good about this."

"You're a credit to the service. Now, get on with charging and remanding those four toe-rags you nicked on the weekend. Leave the rest to me. I'll stay on top of this."

Mike stopped at the door and turned to face his boss. "Sir?"

The ACC nodded.

"The question... about me being unsure?"

He nodded again.

"Yes, on both counts."

28

I felt much better. Molly had made some progress and seemed to be more like her old self, but I knew it would be a long road to full recovery.

With all that had been going on, I felt a bit of a shit. Mike was overseeing Operation Hydra, and I knew for a fact, through years of experience, that it was a very stressful situation. However, he had been assuring me that all was in hand and that the charges were forthcoming

I had a call around midday. It was put through to my office phone.

"DCI Terry McGuire."

I recognised the voice on the other end.

"Terry? It's me, Steve Diamond. Can you speak, are you on your own?"

"Fuck me, Steve, is everything OK?"

Steve chuckled. "You'll never guess who's in the nick with me…"

I wasn't in the mood for games. "Who, Steve? Surprise me," I groaned.

"Cliff Ambrose, that's who. He's been here a few months. He's ruling the roost here, butt. He's still the same, arrogant twat."

I sat up straight. The call had suddenly become very interesting.

"Thought I'd better call you because I've heard

he's out to get you, butt. Rumour is that he wants you topped, and he's put the wheels in motion. He's got some mad Jock by the name of Nevin. I don't know whether it's a load of fanny or straight up, you know what he's like. He's still giving it the big 'I am.' They tell me he hadn't been here a day and he put some so-called hard bloke in the infirmary with a ruptured spleen, broken nose, and other assorted body modifications. You know what it's like in here, it's dog-eat-dog and all that shite."

My blood was at boiling point. Steve had confirmed my theory. Cliff *was* behind it. He was the bastard responsible for Molly being in hospital. I was lost in my thoughts and didn't reply.

"You still there, Terry?"

I gathered my composure and told him about Molly's accident and the severed brake pipes.

"Looks like the Jock is in play, Terry. You be careful. If I get any more information, I'll give you a bell. As for Cliff, he may think he's ruling the roost down here, but I think that'll be coming to an end shortly, if you know what I mean?"

I thanked Steve and put the phone down. I cupped my head in my hands and started cursing. I had to get hold of this Jock before he could complete his mission. I would bury the bastard; I swore to that on my Molly's life.

I had an idea. I rang an old mate of mine, a bloke called Bob who worked in Prison Liaison, and asked him to find out Nevin's full details and if he ever did any of his bird with Cliff.

He assured me I'd have the information within the hour.

I was chomping at the bit, pacing up and down the office. I was tempted to have a glass of malt, but knew I had to keep my head clear.

Mike entered my office and updated me on the op'. I wasn't really listening; my mind was elsewhere.

"You OK, Terry? You seem a bit distant."

"I'm OK, Mike, just thinking about Molly and the kids. They're coming to visit in a few weeks. That'll be great for her. Don't worry about me, you crack on, tell the squad I'm saying, 'well done.'"

I pushed some paper around my desk, even tidied up some of the files I had begun to empty from the boxes and were littering my office floor, when my mate Bob rang. "Got a pen, Terry? This bloke's a nutter with all the screws loose."

"Fire away," I said.

"His name is Alex Nevin. Born 11/08/1955. CRO number is 111223/71. He's got pre-cons for robbery, aggravated burglary with a sawn-off shotgun, some taking and driving without consent, possession of a firearm with intent and a section 18 wounding.

"Shared a cell with Ambrose in Birmingham before Ambrose moved to Swansea and then he was released three months ago."

"Tasty bastard," I said.

"Terry, the bloke is terminally ill, got about twelve months to go."

"Shit. Any release address for him?"

"Yes," Bob said. "Funny thing is, it's down your neck of the woods, Terry, Seabreeze, Mackworth Road, Porthcawl, a halfway house for the DSS and recently released."

I didn't have to write down the address. "I know it."

"Probably wants to die by the seaside, Terry, the smell of fresh air and all that."

"He will fucking die alright, make no bones about that, Bob," I said between gritted teeth. "I owe you one."

I composed myself and thought my birthdays had all come at once. I knew Seabreeze, Mackworth Road very well and I also knew the landlady, Anita Thomas. When I was on division, she was one of my paid informants, officially on the books. She used to have all sorts of people lodging with her. She was a tough cookie. They all had to behave and adhere to her rules, or they were out on their ear. Anita gave me a few cracking cases and was sound as a pound. The last time I saw her was in a fish and chip shop down by Griffin Park a couple of months ago. We had a good chinwag, talked about the old days. She moaned about the young coppers not being like the coppers of the old days and I gave her my direct office number just in case she wanted to rekindle our working relationship.

I gave Anita a ring to see if Nevin was still lodging there. Some of these blokes were like butterflies and bees, they tend to flit all over the place.

I heard the phone ring a few times and a woman answered, I knew it was Anita.

"Anita, it's Terry McGuire, can you talk?"

"Talk of the devil," she said. "Your ears must have been burning. Talking about you a few days ago. What can I do for you?"

"You weren't talking about me to a Jock by the name of Nevin, were you?"

"How do you know that?"

"Is he lodging there with you?"

"Yes. He's been here a couple of months, why? Anything wrong?"

No, not really," I lied. "He's of interest to me and I'd like to give him the old early morning call, you know what I mean?"

She chuckled. "Like the old days, is it, Terry? You're not going bring a bit of excitement into my life at last, are you?"

"Well, I don't know about that, Anita. Tell me, do the same rules apply, front door locked at midnight?"

"Oh yes, Terry, still the same. If they're not in by midnight they sleep in the gutter. Mind you, that's where half of them belong."

I smiled at my end of the line. "What's your

impression of him, Anita?" I knew Anita was a good judge of character, especially those of the criminal kind, she knew a right one from a wrong one.

"Well, to be honest, Terry, he looks like death warmed up, but I wouldn't let that fool you. He gave one of the other lodgers a going over a couple of weeks ago. I reckon he would have killed him, if the others hadn't pulled him off. There's something about him, Terry, it's his eyes, no feeling, cold, stares straight through you. I've got used to all the weird buggers over the years but Nevin makes me feel... uncomfortable. He's not right, not by a long way."

"Any unusual routines?"

"Not really. Never seen him out after 11 p.m. and he keeps himself to himself. Spends most of his time in his room, unless he's having grub with rest of them."

"Which room have you put him in?"

"Number one, at the back, on the ground floor. You know the one; you put the door in often enough. I was sick of seeing that police carpenter, lanky streak of piss."

"I'll be down tonight, just before midnight, to have a little chat with Nevin. Do you still sit in front lounge until they're all stabled?"

"I certainly do, Terry, and it'll be nice to see you, but I'll give you a wide berth when you come, you've got a free hand."

"Cheers, Anita. I knew I could count on you."

I put the phone down. *Right, you Jock bastard, it's either you or me.*

29

After doing the business with Anita, my mind was racing. How would I do this? There was no turning back, I had made my decision. I would have to get rid of Nevin once and for all.

From what I'd been told, Nevin was a psychopath. He hadn't got long to go and by the sounds of it he wanted to go out in a blaze of glory. I could see the headlines now: *'Top Cop slain by deranged gunman in seaside halfway house.'* Well that wasn't going to happen if I planned it right, I would have to make it look like self-defence and I wondered if I should go there tooled up. I could access a firearm, no problem, but then how would I explain that away?

It was highly likely that Nevin would possess a firearm, that was clear from the phone calls. The element of surprise would be my only weapon. I knew the layout of the lodging house. I would have to take my chance.

I gave Mike a shout and told him that I was off to see Molly for a few hours and would then have an early night.

Mike said, "Take a few days off, Terry. Get your head together. Operation Hydra is nearly wrapped up and then when you come back, we will have a full de brief."

"Yes, you're right, Mike, yet again, thank you, that's cracking, butt."

I left and made my way to see Molly. When I arrived at the Intensive Care Unit I was pleasantly surprised to find that Molly had been moved on to one of the general recovery wards.

I enquired with the young nurse and she told me that the consultant had been in earlier and decided that Molly no longer required 24-hour care. I was over the moon.

I made my way to the ward and spoke to the on-duty staff nurse, she directed me to my battered wife.

I entered the ward, and there she was, sitting up, she had earphones in, obviously listening to the radio, she saw me and smiled, and dropped the earphones onto the bedside cabinet.

I gave her a big cwtsh, kissed her and whispered, "I love you, Mols."

"You old softy," she whispered back. We chatted for about three hours, reminiscing about days gone by, the family holidays with the kids, any old rubbish, to be honest, but it was the closest we'd been for a long time. It was amazing how a near death experience could focus the priorities. The thought of losing her had made me sick in my stomach. I finally realised how much she had sacrificed for the bloody job and me. We probably spoke more in that couple of hours than we had in the last three months. That's what the job could do to couples, but Molly knew that.

It must have been 8 pm when I left Molly. She was tired and she needed her rest. I gave her a kiss telling her that all the nonsense would be at an end soon and I would be in to see her tomorrow. But I had my fingers crossed when I said it because, in truth, I wasn't sure if I'd ever get to see her again.

All Molly was concerned about was when I had eaten last, I reassured her that she didn't have to worry and promised I'd call in somewhere for a fish and chip supper.

I hated hospitals, I liked to get out as quickly as I could, but this had been different. This was Molly, my wife and best friend. and I didn't want to leave her there alone.

I finally made for home, I didn't feel hungry, so I gave the chips a miss.

On my way, I drove slowly past Mackworth Road. I couldn't get Nevin out of my mind. His time was coming.

Our home seemed dead, empty of the soul that was Molly. I opened a can of lager and sat and watched a bit of telly, my mind racing, mulling possibilities. I checked my watch; I wanted to get this over with in double quick time.

I didn't really care about my own life; I just wanted an end to all of this for Molly's sake.

At eleven forty, I finally made a move.

I changed into a pair of jogging bottoms and an old rugby jersey and I put on my hardly used trainers. I didn't want to be restricted when the crunch came if I had to grapple with Nevin.

I didn't know what to expect, a sawn-off, a knife, a pistol, perhaps all of those things. I was taking my life in my hands, but I didn't care. I now realised what it felt like to want to kill. Had I gone to the dark side, or was I just simply like any other animal wanting to protect my pack?

I walked. I didn't want my car caught on any CCTV. I made my way down New Road and then cut through the alley by the Spar shop, this took me into Mackworth Road.

'Seabreeze' was just across the street, a large three-storey house, probably built in the fifties. There were a few bedroom lights on, and I could see Anita sitting in the front room. The lounge curtains were wide open, and I could see she was watching TV.

I made my way to the front door and let myself in through the unlocked door. I crept past the lounge, but the door was open, and Anita saw me. She nodded, which I took to be a good sign. Nevin was at home.

As I approached Nevin's room on the ground floor, I could see a strip of light shining under the door. I took a deep breath; my pulse was racing as I stood outside the door. The next few moments would determine the direction of my life. The enormity of what might happen was not lost on me. I had doubts but something inside me kept me rooted to the spot.

This was it.

I booted the door in; it nearly came off the hinges. I burst in and found Nevin lying on the bed. He sprang upright and I could see his skin looked dead, a grey and sallow complexion. He wasn't carrying much weight either. All he was wearing was a pair of grey boxers and a white vest, the skin on his arms looked vacant, as if it had once contained muscles that had now become wasted by the disease.

It's true what they say about moments of life-or-death crisis. The time seemed to slow down, my world had switched to slow-motion mode.

I sailed through the air and landed on top of Nevin. As I screamed at him, even the sounds seemed to be from someplace else, a place where time passed at a leisurely pace. "Try to top me, eh?" my new Barry White voice on thirty-three and a third shouted. I grabbed him by the arms and pulled him off the bed. He didn't say anything, but he struggled, and he franticly kept trying to break free to reach the pillow on the bed. I pulled him to the floor. I punched him in the face several times and I was out of control. I felt the strength drain away from my arms and pulled him closer. I wanted him to see the hatred in my eyes, to feel the loathing and the anger that would result in his end. That was a mistake. He stuck his head to me with incredible force. I knew he'd done my nose. My blood spurted all over the bed.

I was stunned and fell back against the wall opposite the bed. My blood was running back down my throat as I tried to breathe.

Nevin was free and put his hand under the pillow and pulled out a Glock automatic.

He got to his feet and pointed it straight at my forehead, "This is from Cliff," he grinned through battered teeth.

I closed my eyes. I had visions of Molly, the kids, the squad standing by my grave. This was the end.

Then the world returned to normal speed. The room door burst open and I heard a loud voice. "Armed police. Put the gun down..." I opened my eyes and watched Nevin turn away from me to face the officers, gun still in hand.

There were two loud cracks and the room filled with the smell of cordite. Nevin flew backwards through the air and hit the wall. His lifeless body slipped down the white paintwork in a trail of blood and slumped up against me. The firearms officer had done his job with a neat hole in Nevin's chest and another in his throat, the blood pumped out of the holes but I knew it would stop very soon. I knew he was already dead.

"Clear!" the black-clad figure lowered his short barrelled rife.

I got to my feet and held my arms above my head. I wasn't sure if the armed boys were aware that I was a copper, but I wasn't going to take a chance.

I sighed when I saw Mike's face appear behind the armed policeman. "He's ours," he shouted. "He's OK, he's one of us."

I made my way carefully over to him; the blood was still oozing from my nose. Mike gave me his handkerchief to stem the flow. "You stupid bastard, Terry. You could have got yourself killed. What were you thinking, for fuck's sake?"

I sighed and began to shake. "I was thinking too much, Mike."

Mike grabbed me and hugged me for a few moments. "Come on, let's get you cleaned up and processed. This is going to take some explaining. It's a fucking crime scene now."

Mike drove me to the Porthcawl nick where I remained for the next four hours, being attended to by the force doctor and processed by SOCO. I sat quietly throughout. My hands were shaking, not from fear. I had been prepared to face the consequences of my intended actions, but the combination of the adrenalin and realisation of what I might have done was sobering.

I realised that the shit had hit the fan – big time. The only saving grace was the fact that Nevin had been armed and was about to kill me. I was glad. The shooting was lawful and the copper who topped Nevin would be suspended for a while, during the investigation, but would be back to work eventually. I knew the Police Complaints Authority would be involved and there would be an enquiry, but to be honest I didn't really give a shit.

The only thing on my mind was Cliff Ambrose, and how he would react to his hit man, being doubled tapped?

I was nearing the end of my time in the nick when it suddenly hit me. How did Mike and the firearms team get there so quick? My thoughts were interrupted by shouting and screaming from the charge room. It sounded like someone was kicking off – big time. I stepped out of the interview room and walked a few paces around a corner and into the charge room. There, before me, was a scene from one of those Marvel comics. A man-mountain of a guy, stripped to the waist and totally out of control, was throwing coppers around the room as if they were rag dolls. Six burly coppers were clinging to various body parts as the nutter tried to lash out with fists and boots. Then it all made sense. It was the Hulk, one of my detective constables. He was on meltdown.

I was about to join in to help the struggling uniform boys when I saw DS Dai Williams walk in, calm as anything. He took a few moments to measure his response then timed a perfect right hook to the Hulk's face. The big guy crumpled to the charge room floor, unconscious.

Dai saw me. "Got him with enough 'roids to supply the Russian Olympic team," he said.

It took all my self-control not to add a few kicks to the Hulk for good measure. The dull bastard.

30

He sat staring at the screen of a cell phone. The phone was a cheap burner, bought from a convenience store with a pay-as-you-go chip that was practically impossible to trace. Disgraced former Chief Inspector Cliff Ambrose of the South Wales Police drug squad read the text again. He knew what it contained but he couldn't believe it. Nevin was supposed to be the best for the money, a man with nothing to lose, a man with a grudge for coppers he had talked into helping him to get his revenge on the man responsible for putting him behind bars for the rest of his life.

A former colleague had smuggled the phone in to the prison for Ambrose and he had used it sparingly. There were rumours inside that the screws were using a signal detector to pinpoint illegal phones in use but Ambrose knew the routine. He had been told that the scanners weren't used during the changeover of shift and he had another five minutes before the new shift officers would be settled into their duties.

He couldn't believe his eyes. Nevin had failed. Ambrose has paid him twenty grand to do the job on McGuire but had been shot by armed officers in his bail hostel whilst resisting arrest. McGuire had more lives than a bloody cat.

Ambrose should have realised things were not going to end well when Nevin almost killed McGuire's wife. That was not part of the plan. If she had died it might well have been better than killing McGuire himself. The pain and suffering might have driven him over the edge. But that had failed too and Nevin had assured him that he would take McGuire out; shoot him in the leg then in the arm and then in the head, just so he knew what it was like to suffer at the hands of someone who truly hated him.

It had taken Ambrose nearly four weeks to talk Nevin around to taking the hit on McGuire. Nevin hated all cops, him included. But when Ambrose offered him the money and sent the first instalment to Nevin's daughter, he eventually came around.

Nevin had always hated the cops. He had told Ambrose that he had hated them before he was born. His mother and father had been in and out of prison all their lives. Nevin had been born to crime – literally.

At the age of nine, Nevin's father had used him to squeeze through the smallest of windows to break in to homes throughout Glasgow. Being under the age of ten, Nevin's dad had explained that he was under the age of criminal responsibility. If he was caught there was nothing the cops could do. But he wasn't caught. He wasn't caught until he reached the age of twenty-five. He had married a girl from a family that was horrified by her choice of husband. Shona was pregnant with their daughter, Sheena and none of Shona's family would have anything to do with her.

The relationship ended within the year when Nevin was sent down for five years for a series of burglaries that included the homes of Shona's parents and their friends. He had been caught in a house several miles from Shona's family home but knowing he was going to go down, Nevin asked for two dozen other offences to be taken into consideration. It was like a small lottery win for the young Scottish detective dealing with the case and he never had any idea that the true reason for Nevin admitting the other burglaries was his need for Shona's family and their friends to know that he had broken into their homes. He had walked through their kitchens and bedrooms and stolen their jewellery, their money and precious heirlooms.

By that time, his parents were both dead. His mother had died from drinking too much whilst his father had died in a shoot-out with coppers outside a bank in Sterling. The incident had made the national news and Nevin had watched it all with a smile on his face. That was the way to go. It was the only way for someone like his dad and him to die. There was nothing that scared Nevin, nothing other than the thought of growing old and dying in a chair without his mind, dribbling and farting, unable to eat food without dropping it down his front. It wasn't just a fear for him. It was a recurring nightmare.

Neven had not seen Shona and Sheena since he was sent down thirty years ago. He had often wondered how they were getting on. He knew he was a bad man, but he couldn't help thinking about them. He saw it as a weakness and tried to ignore the feelings but as each year passed, he thought more of his daughter. He wondered if she had a good life somewhere. Had she done well in school? Had she become something? Perhaps she had too much of his genes and followed him into crime. Truth was, he had no idea.

He was into a three year stretch for a burglary on a nursing home when the pain in his hips began to become unbearable. It was then he also met Cliff Ambrose. Ambrose was a copper and Nevin did everything he could to get near to him to take a dig at him. He didn't want to kill him, just hurt him enough to know that his life behind bars was never going to get easier. Prison would become his hell on earth.

But Ambrose turned out to be a tough nut. Nevin had watched others have a go at him. Each time, Ambrose would beat back the attacker. Even when three tough inmates tried to get him in the showers, Ambrose kicked and punched and bit and fought with every dirty trick he had. No one seemed to be able to get the better of him and many swore they would do him one day. Nevin knew he could handle Ambrose. But, then the pain in his hips became too much to bear. The prison quack authorised scans on Nevin's hip and within a week he had been diagnosed with stage four bone cancer. He had been given less than a year to live.

It was during that initial period in the prison hospital that Nevin got to speak with Ambrose, Ambrose had been attacked again and had suffered a stab wound to his side. It was nothing serious, Ambrose had told him, but it had earned him a break in the hospital wing.

For some reason, Nevin found himself drawn to Ambrose. The former copper talked openly about his life and what he had done and during one of their conversations Nevin had told him about his wife and daughter. Nevin knew he was going to owe Ambrose when the man offered to use one of his contacts inside the job to find the current whereabouts of Nevin's ex-wife and his daughter.

Ambrose was as good as his word. Shona had died a decade ago but Sheena and her family of two children lived in a small village in Newark in Nottinghamshire. Ambrose had the address and even manged to get a photograph of Sheena, obviously taken from some social network site.

Due to his condition, parole quickly followed,

with conditions. He couldn't reside anywhere near his old stomping ground. Ambrose had suggested a bail hostel in Wales and offered the money for Nevin's daughter if he did one last job before he died.

He had told Ambrose to fuck off, but the nightmare returned that night, the nightmare of sitting in a high-back chair with liver-spotted hands, the smell of urine that he knew was emanating from himself and the patronising smile of the woman spoon-feeding him his dinner. Ambrose's offer suddenly seemed attractive.

But Nevin had failed.

Ambrose hid the phone in a book he had hollowed out for it to fit inside. It was an old trick, something he had seen in some spy movie as a kid. He knew it would be found as soon as the cell was searched but it didn't matter. Phones were ten-a-penny and he could get another just as easily. What would they do to him – extend his sentence? He was already going to serve the rest of his life inside. That was something he didn't want to do. He thought about ways to escape, he had been thinking of ways since he was first held on remand. He missed the outside, the freedom to go where he wanted when he wanted. It had been a freedom he had never truly appreciated but now he did, ever since that freedom had been taken away from him. Perhaps Nevin had felt the same way about his daughter?

Perhaps he had never really appreciated her until he knew he would never see her again?

Life was strange, cruel and fucked up.

31

The ACC hadn't suspended me. That was a pleasant surprise. I had explained that I had had a tipoff from an informant that the person responsible for cutting the brakes of my car was residing at a bail hostel close to my home. I said I just wanted to check it out and that when I got there, I simply wanted to question the suspect, but he ran into his room, and locked the door behind him. I acted on instinct and kicked the door in and then saw him pull a gun on me. We fought but he knocked me back by headbutting me. He was about to pull the trigger when the boys in blue arrived like superheroes.

Of course, some of it was true but most of it wasn't and I guessed that ACC Alan Chambers knew exactly which bits were and which bits weren't. He seemed to accept the story and that was all that mattered. What would an investigation achieve, other than show a previously solid and dependable detective had been pushed to the very edge of his integrity.

I felt bad because I knew that when the chips were down, when my back was to the wall, and any other cliché that applied, I failed to display the level of integrity that I had always expected from others. I had been lucky that it had worked out for me but what about those where perhaps it didn't work out so well. I realised for the first time that life is never black and white. It is a full range of greys that I could now see a lot clearer.

I made it into the office about midday. I was drained but that black cloud that had been hanging over me and Molly had been blown away – literally.

I sat at my desk and noticed smells that I hadn't ever noticed before. I could smell the cardboard of the stacks of case files littering the floor. I could smell the polish on my desk, not that I had ever seen anyone polish it. The leather chair, the paint on the walls, all smelled fresh. I was told by the doctor that I'd probably not be able to smell anything for a few days and I was amazed that I could smell anything at all after the damage I had sustained from Nevin's headbutt. I wondered if my near-death experience had caused an awakening of my senses. Perhaps I was experiencing things differently now? Perhaps I would never see things as I had seen them before? I wondered if that was a good or a bad thing. I would just have to wait and see.

The team office was deserted, except for Jeff. He brought me a coffee. "How are you, boss? Been through the mill, from what we've been told. The boys had no idea how serious things were, sorry."

"Thanks, Jeff, no worries. It was better they didn't know. How are they all doing?"

"No problems, boss. Hydra has given us all a new lease of life and that's down to you and Mike. So, cheers for that."

Jeff returned to his desk. He was a lot like me

in his organisational skills; the desk was littered with folders, covert radios and anything else that couldn't find a place on the floor around it struggled for space on the top alongside the computer and keyboard. I couldn't really tell him to sort it out, not whilst mine looked the same. I watched Jeff sort through a folder and I thought he'd found his calling. He looked content. I thought I'd get him to sort mine out too.

It was a few minutes later and I'd poured Jeff and me another coffee when Mike walked in. He was smiling but looked tired.

"How are you, Terry?"

"All sorted with the local boys," I smiled. "Seems they were happy with my version of events."

"Oh? Gullible, are they?" he sniggered.

"Agatha Christie's got nothing on me, mate," I laughed.

"By fuck, you were lucky last night."

"I know, Mike," I said. It was no laughing matter. "I should have kept you in the loop, but my head had gone, all that business with Molly and Ambrose and Nevin playing out in my head."

Mike collapsed in to my spare chair, clearly wanting to tell me something, when I got a call from the Governor of Swansea nick.

"DCI McGuire?" the Governor said. "I'm just ringing to inform you that Cliff Ambrose is dead."

I was shocked, but also relieved. "What the hell has happened?"

"My officers found him hanging in his cell this morning. He'd ripped and tied some sheets and hanged himself from the upright of the top bunk. He was on his own, so he wasn't found for a few hours. The local officers have dealt with it all and the coroner has been informed. No suspicious circumstances. Hope you don't mind me ringing, chief? But I know there's some history with you."

"That's an understatement. Thanks for letting me know."

I placed the phone back on the charging unit and looked at Mike. "It's really over now, Mike, Ambrose has topped himself in the nick."

"Good enough for the bent bastard. Probably couldn't handle the thought of being stuck behind bars for the rest of his filthy life. Probably only stuck it out this long to take a pop at you. Perhaps now you and Molly can get on with a normal life? Although living with you can't be exactly normal can it?"

We both had a chuckle. I opened the top drawer and pulled out the half full bottle of malt.

Jeff knocked the door and had three clean glasses in his hand. *I was now sure the bastard was psychic.* He handed me the glasses and grinned as I poured him a shot. "Oh, boss, I took the liberty of washing those grubby glasses. There was enough life in there to colonise Mars," he said with a shudder. "Karl was full of smiles yesterday," he continued. "Seems he's had a bit of luck and come into some money." Jeff necked his malt and returned to his desk.

I looked at Mike. "He's not gambling again?"

Mike shook his head. "The Welfare bloke rang the office whilst you were... otherwise indisposed. He wanted me to tell you that the money issue was sorted for Karl, whatever the fuck that meant? I assume that's what Jeff is talking about?"

I poured Mike and me two small ones and we made a toast. "To Just Deserts!"

Mike still looked unsure. He drank his whisky and thumped the glass onto my desk with a clear resolve. Whatever he had to say was about to be said. "I don't know how to say this, but…"

"It's OK, Mike, I know what you're going to say. Don't worry about it. Was it just the two phones?" I had thought about how the firearms team had got to me so quickly and the only answer was an expensive stakeout or phone taps. I didn't think they had any reason for the manpower of a stakeout – I hadn't done anything to warrant that, but phone taps were the only other option.

Mike looked relieved, "Yes, boss, I had a chat with the ACC, I felt I had to. I was worried for you and when Diamond called, I thought it would push you right over the edge. That's when I set up the op' with the firearms team and the local CID. But then you turned up earlier than we thought and it all went tits up. We weren't far behind you. When the landlady ran out screaming and shouting, I sent the two firearm boys in and they were quick, fair play to them. They were in like a dose of salts. When they saw the gun in Nevin's hand there wasn't much they could do. That was it."

Mike stood and poured himself another shot. "I feel terrible, boss. I've betrayed you..." I was shocked as tears started running down his face, he was falling apart.

I got up and grabbed hold of him, gave him a cwtsh like only two Welsh blokes can – arms extended, bottoms pushed out as far from each other as possible and lots of back patting. "You have nothing to feel guilty about, you saved my life. I was out of control, on the edge. I nearly ruined everything, my job, my marriage, and my integrity. I wouldn't have been able to live with that, Mike."

We broke the hug. "I thank you from the bottom of my heart, you're a great friend and half decent detective," I joked. Mike laughed. "I owe you."

We finished our glasses of malt and Mike left, feeling better, I hoped.

I sat back in my chair and felt the tension drain from me. It was over, thank God. I could get back to normality, if there was such a thing for a copper? I had to spend more time at home, looking after Molly and myself. I had to get my head together if I was also going to look after the squad. They deserved that from me too.

The flasher was still at large, and I knew

something had to be done to catch him. Caroline was doing her best, but it was becoming a case that required more resources thrown at it. I blamed myself for taking it all too lightly. Caroline had now seen the bloke's face too but couldn't identify him.

One of the witnesses had said the flasher reminded her of a celebrity but couldn't be sure which one. I wondered if we had some wayward celeb with a penchant for flashing his bits? I didn't think so. But at least we were beginning to get somewhere. We even had the bloke's DNA on file. All we had to do now was make an arrest and test the suspect against the sample already taken. I promised myself that I would do something about the flasher.

I did have a little moment thinking about the death of Ambrose in his cell. I couldn't imagine an arrogant prick like that topping himself. I really didn't think he'd do it. I'd heard of cases where prisoners were topped by others and the scene had been set up to look like suicide or an accident. Ambrose was a former copper – a disgraced one. Prisoners hated coppers almost as much as they hated rapists and paedophiles. The only time they liked coppers was when they nicked rapists and paedophiles.

I couldn't see anything in the personality of Cliff Ambrose that would suggest he would take his own life – nothing. His arrogance and belief that he was better than everyone else made me think he's be more set on finding a way to get out through other means. But, like Steve Diamond said, it's a dog-eat-dog world in the nick. Perhaps he just couldn't take the idea of never being free again? Good enough for the bent bastard.

I grabbed my coat from the rack Molly had bought me for the office. She had grown tired of ironing my suit jackets and ordered me to hang them up instead of draping them over the back of my chair. I had told her that she didn't have to iron my jackets, I was more than capable of doing it myself but then she asked me why I never bothered then? It was a fair point.

I donned my coat and waved at Jeff and Mike who were reading through a page of evidence from the Hydra case.

"I'm going for a walk to clear my head," I said.

They nodded and carried on reading.

I walked out of the station and took a stroll to a nearby coffee shop.

Two young men stood outside the shop. Both puffed on roll-up cigarettes and spoke in hushed tones. They watched me as I strode past. One said, "Alright?"

"Fantastic," I said as I reached the door and entered the shop.

The place was always busy, and it was impossible to get a seat near the window, but I didn't want to sit by the window. I wanted to sit with my back to the wall and just watch the other customers. I ordered my extortionate mug of frothy coffee and took a seat. My handcuff pouch pressed in to my side and I adjusted it without anyone seeing me doing so,

I watched the men and women of all ages sitting and chatting and smiling and frowning. A young woman sat near the door and sipped from a similar mug as mine and rocked the pink pushchair to keep her little girl happy. She had draped her handbag over the handle of the buggy, and I was about to warn her it could be stolen then checked myself. I was overreacting. I was exhausted. It had begun to catch up with me. I'd had a busy few months and I think the pressure of dealing with high profile cases that led to convictions of former colleagues didn't make it any easier. I thought about Molly and how we should visit the kids. I thought about retiring and then perhaps spending six months overseas with the kids.

I knew I was good at my job, but I also knew I couldn't go on forever.

The little girl in the pram seemed content.

I saw the two men from outside the shop open the door and step in.

The coffee tasted good but was too hot to drink much.

I saw the two men stare at the woman with the buggy then I saw one make a snatch at the bag. The woman shrieked and the baby woke and began to scream. The men made a run for the door but weren't quick enough. I might well have been exhausted, I might well be getting older and jaded and missing my wife and kids, but I could still move pretty quickly. My coffee mug was still falling through the air, heading for the inevitable crash into millions of pieces by the time I reached the two men and slammed their heads together.

The mug had just hit the tiled floor when I ripped the bag from the grubby mitt of the thief and threw it back to the young woman.

Millions of pieces of mug did not materialise. The coffee spilled and the mug hit the floor, but it didn't break. Probably some health and safety design that prevented injuries, but it bounced and before it came back to ground for another strike, I had pushed the two men through the door and had cuffed them together.

I looked back at the people in the coffee shop and none of them had reacted to the attempted robbery. None of them had moved. They had looked and they had seen but none of them had done anything. I had reacted out of instinct. I had done what I had been trained to do but I also knew that I would have done it even if I wasn't a copper. Then I realised that I still had value, I still had a job to do and I knew I would continue to do it as long as I was physically and mentally able to do so.

"Right, boys. You're fucking nicked," I said with a smile.

Lightning Source UK Ltd.
Milton Keynes UK
UKHW020706040320
359750UK00012B/1180

9 781789 420678